*She stared up at him in the moonlight.
He stared straight back at her and she
felt her heart surge.*

What am I getting into? she demanded of herself,
but suddenly she didn't care. The night was warm,
the boat was lovely, and this man was holding her
hands, looking down at her in the moonlight. His
hands were imparting strength and surety and
promise.

Promise? What was he promising? She was being
fanciful.

She had to be careful, she told herself fiercely. She
must.

It was too late.

"Yes," she said, before she could change her mind—
and she was committed.

She was heading to the other side of the world with
a man she'd met less than a day ago. Was she out of
her mind?

Do you ever wish you could
step into someone else's shoes?

Now you can, with Harlequin® Romance's miniseries

In Her Shoes

Modern-day Cinderellas get their grooms!

Follow each footstep,
through makeover to marriage, rags to riches,
as these women fulfill their hopes and dreams....

Step into Sarah's red slippers
in this modern-day fairy tale in New York

If the Red Slipper Fits...

By Shirley Jump

October 2010

MARION LENNOX

Cinderella: Hired by the Prince

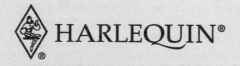

TORONTO • NEW YORK • LONDON
AMSTERDAM • PARIS • SYDNEY • HAMBURG
STOCKHOLM • ATHENS • TOKYO • MILAN • MADRID
PRAGUE • WARSAW • BUDAPEST • AUCKLAND

Recycling programs
for this product may
not exist in your area.

ISBN-13: 978-0-373-17676-2

CINDERELLA: HIRED BY THE PRINCE

First North American Publication 2010.

This edition published by arrangement with Harlequin Books S.A.

For questions and comments about the quality of this book
please contact us at Customer_eCare@Harlequin.ca.

® and TM are trademarks of the publisher. Trademarks indicated with
® are registered in the United States Patent and Trademark Office, the
Canadian Trade Marks Office and in other countries.

www.eHarlequin.com

Printed in U.S.A.

Marion Lennox is a country girl, born on an Australian dairy farm. She moved on—mostly because the cows just weren't interested in her stories! Married to a "very special doctor," Marion writes Medical™ Romances as well as Harlequin® Romance. (She used a different name for each category for a while—if you're looking for her past Harlequin Romances, search for author Trisha David as well.) She's now had more than seventy-five romance novels accepted for publication.

In her non-writing life Marion cares for kids, cats, dogs, chooks and goldfish. She travels, and she fights her rampant garden (she's losing) and her house dust (she's lost).

Having spun in circles for the first part of her life, she's now stepped back from her "other" career, which was teaching statistics at her local university. Finally she's reprioritized her life, figured out what's important and discovered the joys of deep baths, romance and chocolate.

Preferably all at the same time!

'You must marry—everything,' Sofia gave a

PROLOGUE

'RAMÓN spends his life in jeans and ancient T-shirts. He has money and he has freedom. Why would he want the Crown?'

Señor Rodriguez, legal advisor to the Crown of Cepheus, regarded the woman before him with some sympathy. The Princess Sofía had been evicted from the palace of Cepheus sixty years ago, and she didn't wish to be back here now. Her face was tear-stained and her plump hands were wringing.

'I had two brothers, Señor Rodriguez,' she told him, as if explaining her story could somehow alter the inevitable. 'But I was only permitted to know one. My younger brother and I were exiled with my mother when I was ten years old, and my father's cruelty didn't end there. And now... I haven't seen a tiara in sixty years and, as far as I know, Ramón's never seen one. The only time he's been in the palace is the night his father died. I've returned to the palace because my mother raised me with a sense of duty, but how can we demand that from Ramón? To return to the place that killed his father...'

'The Prince Ramón has no choice,' the lawyer said flatly. 'And of course he'll want the Crown.'

'There's no "of course" about it,' Sofía snapped. 'Ramón spends half of every year building houses for some charity in Bangladesh, and the rest of his life on his beautiful yacht. Why should he give that up?'

'He'll be Crown Prince.'

'You think royalty's everything?' Sofía gave up hand

wringing and stabbed at her knitting as if she'd like it to be the late, unlamented Crown Prince. 'My nephew's a lovely young man and he wants nothing to do with the throne. The palace gives him nightmares, as it gives us all.'

'He must come,' Señor Rodriguez said stiffly.

'So how will you find him?' Sofía muttered. 'When he's working in Bangladesh Ramón checks his mail, but for the rest of his life he's around the world in that yacht of his, who knows where? Since his mother and sister died he lets the wind take him where it will. And, even if you do find him, how do you think he'll react to being told he has to fix this mess?'

'There won't be a mess if he comes home. He'll come, as you have come. He must see there's no choice.'

'And what of the little boy?'

'Philippe will go into foster care. There's no choice there, either. The child is nothing to do with Prince Ramón.'

'Another child of no use to the Crown,' Sofía whispered, and she dropped two stiches without noticing. 'But Ramón has a heart. Oh, Ramón, if I were you I'd keep on sailing.'

CHAPTER ONE

'JENNY, lose your muffins. Get a life!'

Gianetta Bertin, known to the Seaport locals as Jenny, gave her best friend a withering look and kept right on spooning double choc chip muffin mixture into pans. Seaport Coffee 'n' Cakes had been crowded all morning, and her muffin tray was almost bare.

'I don't have time for lectures,' she told her friend severely. 'I'm busy.'

'You need to have time for lectures. Honest, Jen.' Cathy hitched herself up onto Jenny's prep bench and grew earnest. 'You can't stay stuck in this hole for ever.'

'There's worse holes to be stuck in, and get off my bench. If Charlie comes in he'll sack me, and I won't have a hole at all.'

'He won't,' Cathy declared. 'You're the best cook in Seaport. You hold this place up. Charlie's treating you like dirt, Jen, just because you don't have the energy to do anything about it. I know you owe him, but you could get a job and repay him some other way.'

'Like how?' Jenny shoved the tray into the oven, straightened and tucked an unruly curl behind her ear. Her cap was supposed to hold back her mass of dark curls, but they kept escaping. She knew she'd now have a streak of flour across her ear but did it matter what she looked like?

And, as if in echo, Cathy continued. 'Look at you,' she

declared. 'You're gorgeous. Twenty-nine, figure to die for, cute as a button, a woman ripe and ready for the world, and here you are, hidden in a shapeless white pinafore with flour on your nose—yes, flour on your nose, Jen—no don't wipe it, you've made it worse.'

'It doesn't matter,' Jenny said. 'Who's looking? Can I get on? There's customers out there.'

'There are,' Cathy said warmly, peering out through the hatch but refusing to let go of her theme. 'You have twenty people out there, all coming here for one of your yummy muffins and then heading off again for life. You should be out there with them. Look at that guy out there, for instance. Gorgeous or what? That's what you're missing out on, Jen, stuck in here every day.'

Jenny peered out the hatch as well, and it didn't take more than a glance to see who Cathy was referring to.

The guy looked to be in his mid-thirties. He was a yachtie—she could tell that by his gear—and he was seriously good-looking. It had been raining this morning. He was wearing battered jeans, salt-stained boating shoes and a faded black T-shirt, stretched tight over a chest that looked truly impressive. He'd shrugged a battered sou'wester onto the back of his chair.

Professional, she thought.

After years of working in Coffee 'n' Cakes she could pick the classes of boaty. Holding the place up were the hard-core fishermen. Then there were the battered old salts who ran small boats on the smell of an oily rag, often living on them. Next there was the cool set, arriving at weekends, wearing gear that came out of the designer section of the *Nautical Monthly* catalogue, and leaving when they realized Coffee 'n' Cakes didn't sell Chardonnay.

And finally there were the serious yachties. Seaport was a deep water harbour just south of Sydney, and it attracted yachts doing amazing journeys. Seaport had a great dry dock where repairs could be carried out expertly and fast, so there were often one or two of these classy yachts in port.

This guy looked as if he was from one of these. His coat looked battered but she knew the brand, even from this distance. It was the best. Like the man. The guy himself also looked a bit battered, but in a good way. Worn by the sea. His tan was deep and real, his eyes were crinkled as if he spent his life in the sun, and his black hair was only really black at the roots. The tips were sun-bleached to almost fair.

He was definitely a professional sailor, she thought, giving herself a full minute to assess him. And why not? He was well worth assessing.

She knew the yachting hierarchy. The owners of the big sea-going yachts tended to be middle-aged or older. They spent short bursts of time on their boats but left serious seafaring to paid staff. This guy looked younger, tougher, leaner than a boat-owner. He looked seriously competent. He'd be being paid to take a yacht to where its owner wanted it to be.

And for a moment—just for a moment—Jenny let herself be consumed by a wave of envy. Just to go where the wind took you… To walk away from Seaport…

No. That'd take effort and planning and hope—all the things she no longer cared about. And there was also debt, an obligation like a huge anchor chained around her waist, hauling her down.

But her friend was thinking none of these things. Cathy was prodding her, grinning, rolling her eyes at the sheer good looks of this guy, and Jenny smiled and gazed a little bit more. Cathy was right—this guy was definite eye-candy. What was more, he was munching on one of her muffins—lemon and pistachio. Her favourite, she thought in approval.

And then he looked up and saw her watching. He grinned and raised his muffin in silent toast, then chuckled as she blushed deep crimson and pushed the hatch closed.

Cathy laughed her delight. 'There,' she said in satisfaction. 'You see what's out there? He's gorgeous, Jen. Why don't you head on out and ask him if he'd like another muffin?'

'As if,' she muttered, thoroughly disconcerted. She shoved

her mixing bowl into the sink. 'Serving's Susie's job. I'm just the cook. Go away, Cathy. You're messing with my serenity.'

'Stuff your serenity,' Cathy said crudely. 'Come on, Jen. It's been two years…' Then, as she saw the pain wash across Jenny's face, she swung herself off the bench and came and hugged her. 'I know. Moving on can't ever happen completely, but you can't keep hiding.'

'Dr Matheson says I'm doing well,' Jenny said stubbornly.

'Yeah, he's prescribing serenity,' Cathy said dourly. 'Honey, you've had enough peace. You want life. Even sailing… You love the water, but now you don't go near the sea. There's so many people who'd like a weekend crew. Like the guy out there, for instance. If he offered me a sail I'd be off for more than a weekend.'

'I don't want…'

'Anything but to be left alone,' Cathy finished for her. 'Oh, enough. I won't let you keep on saying it.' And, before Jenny could stop her, she opened the hatch again. She lifted the bell Jenny used to tell Susie an order was ready and rang it like there was a shipwreck in the harbour. Jenny made a grab for it but Cathy swung away so her body protected the bell. Then, when everyone was watching…

'Attention, please,' she called to the room in general, in the booming voice she used for running the Seaport Ladies' Yoga Sessions. 'Ladies and gentlemen, I know this is unusual but I'd like to announce a fantastic offer. Back here in the kitchen is the world's best cook and the world's best sailor. Jenny's available as crew for anyone offering her excitement, adventure and a way out of this town. All she needs is a fantastic wage and a boss who appreciates her. Anyone interested, apply right here, right now.'

'Cathy!' Jenny stared at her friend in horror. She made a grab for the hatch doors and tugged them shut as Cathy collapsed into laughter. 'Are you out of your mind?'

'I love you, sweetheart,' Cathy said, still chuckling. 'I'm just trying to help.'

'Getting me sacked won't help.'

'Susie won't tell Charlie,' Cathy said. 'She agrees with me. Don't you, Susie?' she demanded as the middle-aged waitress pushed her way through the doors. 'Do we have a queue out there, Suse, all wanting to employ our Jen?'

'You shouldn't have done it,' Susie said severely, looking at Jenny in concern. 'You've embarrassed her to death.'

'There's no harm done,' Cathy said. 'They're all too busy eating muffins to care. But honest, Jen, put an ad in the paper, or at least start reading the Situations Vacant. Susie has a husband, four kids, two dogs and a farm. This place is a tiny part of her life. But for you… This place has become your life. You can't let it stay that way.'

'It's all I want,' Jenny said stubbornly. 'Serenity.'

'That's nonsense,' Susie declared.

'Of course it's nonsense,' Cathy said, jumping off the bench and heading for the door. 'Okay, Stage One of my quest is completed. If it doesn't have an effect then I'll move to Stage Two, and that could be really scary.'

Coffee 'n' Cakes was a daytime café. Charlie was supposed to lock up at five, but Charlie's life was increasingly spent in the pub, so at five Jenny locked up, as she was starting to do most nights.

At least Charlie hadn't heard of what had happened that morning. Just as well, Jenny thought as she turned towards home. For all Cathy's assurances that she wouldn't be sacked, she wasn't so sure. Charlie's temper was unpredictable and she had debts to pay. Big debts.

Once upon a time Charlie had been a decent boss. Then his wife died, and now…

Loss did ghastly things to people. It had to her. Was living in a grey fog of depression worse than spending life in an alcoholic haze? How could she blame Charlie when she wasn't much better herself?

She sighed and dug her hands deep into her jacket pockets. The rain from this morning had disappeared. It was warm enough, but she wanted the comfort of her coat. Cathy's behaviour had unsettled her.

She would've liked to take a walk along the harbour before she went home, only in this mood it might unsettle her even more.

All those boats, going somewhere.

She had debts to pay. She was going nowhere.

'Excuse me?'

The voice came from behind her. She swung around and it was him. The guy with the body, and with the smile.

Okay, that was a dumb thing to think, but she couldn't help herself. The combination of ridiculously good-looking body and a smile to die for meant it was taking everything she had not to drop her jaw.

It had been too long, she thought. No one since...

No. Don't even think about going there.

'Can I talk to you? Are you Jenny?'

He had an accent—Spanish maybe, she thought, and seriously sexy. Uh oh. Body of a god, killer smile and a voice that was deep and lilting and gorgeous. Her knees felt wobbly. Any minute now he'd have her clutching the nearest fence for support.

Hey! She was a grown woman, she reminded herself sharply. Where was a bucket of ice when she needed one? Making do as best she could, she tilted her chin, met his gaze square on and fought for composure.

'I'm Jenny.' Infuriatingly, her words came out a squeak. She turned them into a cough and tried again. 'I...sure.'

'The lady in the café said you were interested in a job,' he said. 'I'm looking for help. Can we talk about it?'

He was here to offer her a job?

His eyes were doing this assessing thing while he talked. She was wearing old jeans and an ancient duffel, built for service rather than style. Was he working out where she fitted in the social scale? Was he working out whether she cared what she wore?

Suddenly she found herself wishing she had something else on. Something with a bit of…glamour?

Now that was crazy. She was heading home to put her feet up, watch the telly and go to bed. What would she do with glamour?

He was asking her about a job. Yeah, they all needed deckhands, she thought, trying to ground herself. Lots of big yachts came into harbour here. There'd be one guy in charge—someone like this. There'd also be a couple of deckies, but the guy in charge would be the only one paid reasonable wages by the owners. Deckies were to be found in most ports—kids looking for adventure, willing to work for cheap travel. They'd get to their destination and disappear to more adventure, to be replaced by others.

Did this man seriously think she might be interested in such a job?

'My friend was having fun at my expense,' she said, settling now she knew what he wanted. Still trying to firm up her knees, though. 'Sorry, but I'm a bit old to drop everything and head off into the unknown.'

'Are you ever too old to do that?'

'Yes,' she snapped before she could stop herself—and then caught herself. 'Sorry. Look, I need to get on.'

'So you're not interested.'

'There's a noticeboard down at the yacht club,' she told him. 'There's always a list of kids looking for work. I already have a job.'

'You do have a job.' His smile had faded. He'd ditched his coat, leaving only his jeans and T-shirt. They were faded and old and…nice. He was tall and broad-shouldered. He looked loose-limbed, casually at ease with himself and quietly confident. His eyes were blue as the sea, though they seemed to darken when he smiled, and the crinkles round his eyes said smiling was what he normally did. But suddenly he was serious.

'If you made the muffins I ate this morning you're very,

very good at your job,' he told her. 'If you're available as crew, a man'd be crazy not to take you on.'

'Well, I'm not.' He had her rattled and she'd snapped again. Why? He was a nice guy offering her a job. 'Sorry,' she said. 'But no.'

'Do you have a passport?'

'Yes, but…'

'I'm sailing for Europe just as soon as I can find some company. It's not safe to do a solo where I'm going.'

'Round the Horn?' Despite herself, she was interested.

'Round the Horn,' he agreed. 'It's fastest.'

That'd be right. The boaties in charge of the expensive yachts were usually at the call of owners. She'd met enough of them to know that. An owner fancied a sailing holiday in Australia? He'd pay a guy like this to bring his boat here and have it ready for him. Maybe he'd join the boat on the interesting bits, flying in and out at will. Now the owner would be back in Europe and it'd be up to the employed skipper—this guy?—to get the boat back there as soon as he could.

With crew. But not with her.

'Well, good luck,' she said, and started to walk away, but he wasn't letting her leave. He walked with her.

'It's a serious offer.'

'It's a serious rejection.'

'I don't take rejection kindly.'

'That's too bad,' she told him. 'The days of carting your crew on board drugged to the eyeballs is over. Press gangs are illegal.'

'They'd make my life easier,' he said morosely.

'You know I'm very sure they wouldn't.' His presence as he fell into step beside her was making her thoroughly disconcerted. 'Having a press-ganged crew waking up with hangovers a day out to sea surely wouldn't make for serene sailing.'

'I don't look for serenity,' he said, and it was so much an echo of her day's thoughts that she stopped dead.

But this was ridiculous. The idea was ridiculous. 'Serenity's important,' she managed, forcing her feet into moving again. 'So thank you, but I've said no. Is there anything else you want?'

'I pay well.'

'I know what deckies earn.'

'You don't know what I pay. Why don't you ask?'

'I'm not interested.'

'Do you really sail?' he asked curiously.

He wasn't going away. She was quickening her steps but he was keeping up with ease. She had the feeling if she broke into a run he'd keep striding beside her, effortlessly. 'Once upon a time, I sailed,' she said. 'Before life got serious.'

'Your life got serious? How?' Suddenly his eyes were creasing in concern. He paused and, before she could stop him, he lifted her left hand. She knew what he was looking for.

No ring.

'You have a partner?' he demanded.

'It's none of your business.'

'Yes, but I want to know,' he said in that gorgeous accent, excellent English but with that fabulous lilt—and there was that smile again, the smile she knew could get him anything he wanted if he tried hard enough. With these looks and that smile and that voice... Whew.

No. He couldn't get anything from her. She was impervious.

She had to be impervious.

But he was waiting for an answer. Maybe it wouldn't hurt to tell him enough to get him off her back. 'I'm happily single,' she said.

'Ah, but if you're saying life's serious then you're not so happily single. Maybe sailing away on the next tide could be just what you want.'

'Look,' she said, tugging her hand away, exasperated. 'I'm not a teenager looking for adventure. I have obligations here. So you're offering me a trip to Europe? Where would that leave me? I'd get on your boat, I'd work my butt off for passage—I know you guys get your money's worth from the kids you employ—and then I'd end up wherever it is you're going. That's it. I know how it works. I wouldn't even have the fare home. I'm not a backpacker, Mr Whoever-You-Are, and I live here. I don't know you, I don't trust you and I'm not interested in your job.'

'My name's Ramón Cavellero,' he said, sounding not in the least perturbed by her outburst. 'I'm very trustworthy.' And he smiled in a way that told her he wasn't trustworthy in the least. 'I'm sailing on the *Marquita*. You've seen her?'

Had she seen her? Every person in Seaport had seen the *Marquita*. The big yacht's photograph had been on the front of their local paper when she'd come into port four days ago. With good reason. Quite simply she was the most beautiful boat Jenny had ever seen.

And probably the most expensive.

If this guy was captaining the *Marquita* then maybe he had the funds to pay a reasonable wage. That was an insidious little whisper in her head, but she stomped on it before it had a chance to grow. There was no way she could walk away from this place. Not for years.

She had to be sensible.

'Look, Mr Cavellero, this has gone far enough,' she said, and she turned back to face him directly. 'You have the most beautiful boat in the harbour. You can have your pick of any deckie in the market—I know a dozen kids at least who would kill to be on that boat. But, as for me… My friend was making a joke but that's all it was. Thank you and goodbye.'

She reached out and took his hand, to give it a good firm handshake, as if she was a woman who knew how to transact business, as if she should be taken seriously. He took it, she shook, but, instead of pulling away after one brief shake, she found he was holding on.

Or maybe it was that she hadn't pulled back as she'd intended.

His hand was strong and warm and his grip as decisive

as hers. Or more. Two strong wills, she thought fleetingly, but more...

But then, before she could think any further, she was aware of a car sliding to a halt beside them. She glanced sideways and almost groaned.

Charlie.

She could sense his drunkenness from here. One of these days he'd be caught for drink-driving, she thought, and half of her hoped it'd be soon, but the other half knew that'd put her boss into an even more foul mood than he normally was. Once upon a time he'd been a nice guy—but that was when he was sober, and she could barely remember when he'd been sober. So she winced and braced herself for an explosion as Charlie emerged from the car and headed towards them.

Ramón kept on holding her hand. She tugged it back and he released her but he shifted in closer. Charlie's body language was aggressive. He was a big man; he'd become an alcoholic bully, and it showed.

But, whatever else Ramón might be, it was clear he knew how to protect his own. His own? That was a dumb thing to think. Even so, she was suddenly glad that he was here right now.

'Hey, I want to speak to you, you stupid cow. Lose your friend,' Charlie spat at her.

Jenny flinched. Uh oh. This could mean only one thing—that one of the patrons of the café had told Charlie of Cathy's outburst. This was too small a town for such a joke to go unreported. Charlie had become universally disliked and the idea that one of his staff was advertising for another job would be used against him.

At her expense.

And Ramón's presence here would make it worse. Protective or not, Charlie was right; she needed to lose him.

'See you later,' she said to Ramón, stepping deliberately away and turning her back on him. Expecting him to leave. 'Hello, Charlie.'

But Charlie wasn't into greetings. 'What the hell do you

think you're doing, making personal announcements in my café, in my time?' He was close to yelling, shoving right into her personal space so she was forced to step backward. 'And getting another job? You walk away from me and I foreclose before the day's end. You know what you owe me, girl. You work for me for the next three years or I'll have you bankrupt and your friend with you. I could toss you out now. Your friend'll lose her house. Great mess that'd leave her in. You'll work the next four weekends with no pay to make up for this or you're out on your ear. What do you say to that?'

She closed her eyes. Charlie was quite capable of carrying out his threats. This man was capable of anything.

Why had she ever borrowed money from him?

Because she'd been desperate, that was why. It had been right at the end of Matty's illness. She'd sold everything, but there was this treatment... There'd been a chance. It was slim, she'd known, but she'd do anything.

She'd been sobbing, late at night, in the back room of the café. She'd been working four hours a day to pay her rent. The rest of the time she'd spent with Matty. Cathy had found her there, and Charlie came in and found them both.

He'd loan her the money, he said, and the offer was so extraordinary both women had been rendered almost speechless.

Jenny could repay it over five years, he'd told them, by working for half wages at the café. Only he needed security. 'In case you decide to do a runner.'

'She'd never do a runner,' Cathy had said, incensed. 'When Matty's well she'll settle down and live happily ever after.'

'I don't believe in happy ever after,' Charlie had said. 'I need security.'

'I'll pledge my apartment that she'll repay you,' Cathy had said hotly. 'I trust her, even if you don't.'

What a disaster. They'd been so emotional they hadn't thought it through. All Jenny had wanted was to get back to the hospital, to get back to Matty, and she didn't care how. Cathy's generosity was all she could see.

So she'd hugged her and accepted and didn't see the ties.

Only ties there were. Matty died a month later and she was faced with five years bonded servitude.

Cathy's apartment had been left to her by her mother. It was pretty and neat and looked out over the harbour. Cathy was an artist. She lived hand to mouth and her apartment was all she had.

Even Cathy hadn't realised how real the danger of foreclosure was, Jenny thought dully. Cathy had barely glanced at the loan documents. She had total faith in her friend to repay her loan. Of course she had.

So now there was no choice. Jenny dug her hands deep into her pockets, she bit back angry words, as she'd bitten them back many times before, and she nodded.

'Okay. I'm sorry, Charlie. Of course I'll do the weekends.'

'Hey!' From behind them came Ramón's voice, laced with surprise and the beginnings of anger. 'What is this? Four weekends to pay for two minutes of amusement?'

'It's none of your business,' Charlie said shortly. 'Get lost.'

'If you're talking about what happened at the café, I was there. It was a joke.'

'I don't do jokes. Butt out. And she'll do the weekends. She has no choice.'

And then he smiled, a drunken smile that made her shiver. 'So there's the joke,' he jeered. 'On you, woman, not me.'

And that was that. He stared defiance at Ramón, but Ramón, it seemed, was not interested in a fight. He gazed blankly back at him, and then watched wordlessly as Charlie swung himself unsteadily back into his car and weaved off into the distance.

Leaving silence.

How to explain what had just happened? Jenny thought, and decided she couldn't. She took a few tentative steps away, hoping Ramón would leave her to her misery.

He didn't. Instead, he looked thoughtfully at the receding car, then flipped open his cellphone and spoke a few sharp words. He snapped it shut and walked after Jenny, catching up and once again falling into step beside her.

'How much do you owe him?' he asked bluntly.

She looked across at him, startled. 'Sorry?'

'You heard. How much?'

'I don't believe that it's...'

'Any of my business,' he finished for her. 'Your boss just told me that. But, as your future employer, I can make it my business.'

'You're not my future employer.'

'Just tell me, Jenny,' he said, and his voice was suddenly so concerned, so warm, so laced with caring that, to her astonishment, she found herself telling him. Just blurting out the figure, almost as if it didn't matter.

He thought about it for a moment as they kept walking. 'That's not so much,' he said cautiously.

'To you, maybe,' she retorted. 'But to me... My best friend signed over her apartment as security. If I don't pay, then she loses her home.'

'You could get another job. You don't have to be beholden to this swine-bag. You could transfer the whole loan to the bank.'

'I don't think you realise just how broke I am,' she snapped and then she shook her head, still astounded at how she was reacting to him. 'Sorry. There's no need for me to be angry with you when you're being nice. I'm tired and I'm upset and I've got myself into a financial mess. The truth is that I don't even have enough funds to miss a week's work while I look for something else, and no bank will take me on. Or Cathy either, for that matter—she's a struggling painter and has nothing but her apartment. So there you go. That's why I work for Charlie. It's also why I can't drop everything and sail away with you. If you knew how much I'd love to...'

'Would you love to?' He was studying her intently. The concern was still there but there was something more. It was as if he was trying to make her out. His brow was furrowed in concentration. 'Would you really? How good a sailor are you?'

That was a weird question but it was better than talking

about her debts. So she told him that, too. Why not? 'I was born and bred on the water,' she told him. 'My dad built a yacht and we sailed it together until he died. In the last few years of his life we lived on board. My legs are more at home at sea than on land.'

'Yet you're a cook.'

'There's nothing like spending your life in a cramped galley to make you lust after proper cooking.' She gave a wry smile, temporarily distracted from her bleakness. 'My mum died early so she couldn't teach me, but I longed to cook. When I was seventeen I got an apprenticeship with the local baker. I had to force Dad to keep the boat in port during my shifts.'

'And your boat? What was she?'

'A twenty-five footer, fibreglass, called *Wind Trader*. Flamingo, if you know that class. She wasn't anything special but we loved her.'

'Sold now to pay debts?' he asked bluntly.

'How did you know?' she said, crashing back to earth. 'And, before you ask, I have a gambling problem.'

'Now why don't I believe that?'

'Why would you believe anything I tell you?' She took a deep breath. 'Look, this is dumb. I'm wrecked and I need to go home. Can we forget we had this conversation? It was crazy to tell you my troubles and I surely don't expect you to do anything about them. But thank you for letting me talk.'

She hesitated then. For some reason, it was really hard to walk away from this man, but she had no choice. 'Goodbye, Mr Cavellero,' she managed. 'Thank you for thinking of me as a potential deckhand. It was very nice of you, and you know what? If I didn't have this debt I'd be half tempted to take it on.'

Once more she turned away. She walked about ten steps, but then his voice called her back.

'Jenny?'

She should have just kept on walking, but there was something in his voice that stopped her. It was the concern again. He sounded as if he really cared.

That was crazy, but the sensation was insidious, like a siren song forcing her to turn around.

'Yes?'

He was standing where she'd left him. Just standing. Behind him, down the end of the street, she could see the harbour. That was where he belonged, she thought. He was a man of the sea. He looked a man from the sea. Whereas she…

'Jenny, I'll pay your debts,' he said.

She didn't move. She didn't say anything.

She didn't know what to say.

'This isn't charity,' he said quickly as she felt her colour rise. 'It's a proposition.'

'I don't understand.'

'It's a very sketchy proposition,' he told her. 'I've not had time to work out the details so we may have to smooth it off round the edges. But, essentially, I'll pay your boss out if you promise to come and work with me for a year. You'll be two deckies instead of one—crew when I need it and cook for the rest of the time. Sometimes you'll be run off your feet but mostly not. I'll also add a living allowance,' he said and he mentioned a sum that made her feel winded.

'You'll be living on the boat so that should be sufficient,' he told her, seemingly ignoring her amazement. 'Then, at the end of the year, I'll organise you a flight home, from wherever *Marquita* ends up. So how about it, Jenny?' And there was that smile again, flashing out to warm parts of her she hadn't known had been cold. 'Will you stay here as Charlie's unpaid slave, or will you come with me, cook your cakes on my boat and see the world? What do you say? *Marquita*'s waiting, Jenny. Come sail away.'

'It's three years' debt,' she gasped finally. Was he mad?

'Not to me. It's one year's salary for a competent cook and sailor, and it's what I'm offering.'

'Your owner could never give the authority to pay those kind of wages.'

He hesitated for a moment—for just a moment—but then he smiled. 'My owner doesn't interfere with how I run my boat,' he told her. 'My owner knows if I…if he pays peanuts, he gets monkeys. I want good and loyal crew and with you I believe I'd be getting it.'

'You don't even know me. And you're out of your mind. Do you know how many deckies you could get with that money?'

'I don't want deckies. I want you.' And then, as she kept right on staring, he amended what had been a really forceful statement. 'If you can cook the muffins I had this morning you'll make my life—and everyone else who comes onto the boat—a lot more pleasant.'

'Who does the cooking now?' She was still fighting for breath. What an offer!

'Me or a deckie,' he said ruefully. 'Not a lot of class.'

'I'd…I'd be expected to cook for the owner?'

'Yes.'

'Dinner parties?'

'There's not a lot of dinner parties on board the *Marquita*,' he said, sounding a bit more rueful. 'The owner's pretty much like me. A retiring soul.'

'You don't look like a retiring soul,' she retorted, caught by the sudden flash of laughter in those blue eyes.

'Retiring or not, I still need a cook.'

Whoa… To be a cook on a boat… With this man…

Then she caught herself. For a moment she'd allowed herself to be sucked in. To think *what if*.

What if she sailed away?

Only she'd jumped like this once before, and where had it got her? Matty, and all the heartbreak that went with him.

Her thoughts must have shown on her face. 'What is it?' Ramón asked, and his smile suddenly faded. 'Hey, Jenny, don't look like that. There's no strings attached to this offer. I swear you won't find yourself the seventeenth member of my harem, chained up for my convenience in the hold. I can even give you character references if you want. I'm extremely honourable.'

He was trying to make her smile. She did smile, but it was a wavery smile. 'I'm sure you're honourable,' she said—despite the laughter lurking behind his amazing eyes suggesting he was nothing of the kind—'but, references or not, I still don't know you.' Deep breath. *Be sensible.* 'Sorry,' she managed. 'It's an amazing offer, but I took a loan from Charlie when I wasn't thinking straight, and look where that got me. And there have been…other times…when I haven't thought straight either, and trouble's followed. So I don't act on impulse any more. I've learned to be sensible. Thank you for your offer, Mr Cavellero…'

'Ramón.'

'Mr Cavellero,' she said stubbornly. 'With the wages you're offering, I know you'll find just the crew you're looking for, no problem at all. So thank you again and goodnight.'

Then, before she could let her treacherous heart do any more impulse urging—before she could be as stupid as she'd been in the past—she turned resolutely away.

She walked straight ahead and she didn't look back.

CHAPTER TWO

HER heart told her she was stupid all the way home. Her head told her she was right.

Her head addressed her heart with severity. This was a totally ridiculous proposition. She didn't know this man.

She'd be jumping from the frying pan into the fire, she told herself. To be indebted to a stranger, then sail away into the unknown... He *could* be a white slave trader!

She knew he wasn't. Take a risk, her heart was commanding her, but then her heart had let her down before. She wasn't going down that road again.

So, somehow, she summoned the dignity to keep on walking.

'Think about it,' Ramón called after her and she almost hesitated, she almost turned back, only she was a sensible woman now, not some dumb teenager who'd jump on the nearest boat and head off to sea.

So she walked on. Round the next corner, and the next, past where Charlie lived.

A police car was pulled up beside Charlie's front door, and Charlie hadn't made it inside. Her boss was being breathalysed. He'd be way over the alcohol limit. He'd lose his licence for sure.

She thought back and remembered Ramón lifting his cellphone. Had he...

Whoa. She scuttled past, feeling like a guilty rabbit.

Ramón had done it, not her.

Charlie would guess. Charlie would never forgive her.

Uh oh, uh oh, uh oh.

By the time she got home she felt as if she'd forgotten to breathe. She raced up the steps into her little rented apartment and she slammed the door behind her.

What had Ramón done? Charlie, without his driving licence? Charlie, thinking it was her fault?

But suddenly she wasn't thinking about Charlie. She was thinking about Ramón. Numbly, she crossed to the curtains and drew them aside. Just checking. Just in case he'd followed. He hadn't and she was aware of a weird stab of disappointment.

Well, what did you expect? she told herself. I told him press gangs don't work.

What if they did? What if he came up here in the dead of night, drugged her and carted her off to sea? What if she woke on his beautiful yacht, far away from this place?

I'd be chained to the sink down in the galley, she told herself with an attempt at humour. Nursing a hangover from the drugs he used to get me there.

But oh, to be on that boat…

He'd offered to pay all her bills. Get her away from Charlie…

What was she about, even beginning to think about such a crazy offer? If he was giving her so much money, then he'd be expecting something other than the work a deckie did.

But a man like Ramón wouldn't have to pay, she thought, her mind flashing to the nubile young backpackers she knew would jump at the chance to be crew to Ramón. They'd probably jump at the chance to be anything else. So why did he want her?

Did he have a thing for older women?

She stared into the mirror and what she saw there almost made her smile. It'd be a kinky man who'd desire her like she was. Her hair was still flour-streaked from the day. She'd been working in a hot kitchen and she'd been washing up over steaming sinks. She didn't have a spot of make-up on, and her nose was shiny. *Very* shiny.

Her clothes were ancient and nondescript and her eyes were shadowed from lack of sleep. Oh, she had plenty of time for sleep, but where was sleep when you needed it? She'd stopped taking the pills her doctor prescribed. She was trying desperately to move on, but how?

'What better way than to take a chance?' she whispered to her image. 'Charlie's going to be unbearable to work with now. And Ramón's gorgeous and he seems really nice. His boat's fabulous. He's not going to chain me to the galley, I'm sure of it.' She even managed a smile at that. 'If he does, I won't be able to help him with the sails. He'd have to unchain me a couple of times a day at least. And I'd be at sea. At sea!'

So maybe…maybe…

Her heart and head were doing battle but her heart was suddenly in the ascendancy. It was trying to convince her it could be sensible as well.

Wait, she told herself severely. She ran a bath and wallowed and let her mind drift. Pros and cons. Pros and cons.

If it didn't work, she could get off the boat at New Zealand.

He'd demand his money back.

So? She'd then owe money to Ramón instead of to Charlie, and there'd be no threat to Cathy's apartment. The debt would be hers and hers alone.

That felt okay. Sensible, even. She felt a prickle of pure excitement as she closed her eyes and sank as deep as she could into the warm water. To sail away with Ramón…

Her eyes flew open. She'd been stupid once. One gorgeous sailor, and…Matty.

So I'm not that stupid, she told herself. I can take precautions before I go.

Before she went? This wasn't turning out to be a relaxing bath. She sat bolt upright in the bath and thought, *what am I thinking*?

She was definitely thinking of going.

'You told him where to go to find deckies,' she said out loud. 'He'll have asked someone else by now.'

No!

'So get up, get dressed and go down to that boat. Right now, before you chicken out and change your mind.

'You're nuts.

'So what can happen that's worse than being stuck here?' she told herself and got out of the bath and saw her very pink body in the mirror. Pink? The sight was somehow a surprise.

For the last two years she'd been feeling grey. She'd been concentrating on simply putting one foot after another, and sometimes even that was an effort.

And now…suddenly she felt pink.

'So go down to the docks, knock on the hatch of Ramón's wonderful boat and say—yes, please, I want to come with you, even if you are a white slave trader, even if I may be doing the stupidest thing of my life. Jumping from the frying pan into the fire? Maybe, but, crazy or not, I want to jump,' she told the mirror.

And she would.

'You're a fool,' she told her reflection, and her reflection agreed.

'Yes, but you're not a grey fool. Just do it.'

What crazy impulse had him offering a woman passage on his boat? A needy woman. A woman who looked as if she might cling.

She was right, he needed a couple of deckies, kids who'd enjoy the voyage and head off into the unknown as soon as he reached the next port. Then he could find more.

But he was tired of kids. He'd been starting to think he'd prefer to sail alone, only *Marquita* wasn't a yacht to sail by himself. She was big and old-fashioned and her sails were heavy and complicated. In good weather one man might manage her, but Ramón didn't head into good weather. He didn't look for storms but he didn't shy away from them either.

The trip back around the Horn would be long and tough, and he'd hardly make it before he was due to return to Bangladesh. He'd been looking forward to the challenge, but at the same time not looking forward to the complications crew could bring.

The episode in the café this morning had made him act on impulse. The woman—Jenny—looked light years from the kids he generally employed. She looked warm and homely and mature. She also looked as if she might have a sense of humour and, what was more, she could cook.

He could make a rather stodgy form of paella. He could cook a steak. Often the kids he employed couldn't even do that.

He was ever so slightly over paella.

Which was why the taste of Jenny's muffins, the cosiness of her café, the look of her with a smudge of flour over her left ear, had him throwing caution to the winds and offering her a job. And then, when he'd realised just where that bully of a boss had her, he'd thrown in paying off her loan for good measure.

Sensible? No. She'd looked at him as if she suspected him of buying her for his harem, and he didn't blame her.

It was just as well she hadn't accepted, he told himself. Move on.

It was time to eat. Maybe he could go out to one of the dockside hotels.

He didn't feel like it. His encounter with Jenny had left him feeling strangely flat—as if he'd seen something he wanted but he couldn't have it.

That made him sound like his Uncle Iván, he thought ruefully. Iván, Crown Prince of Cepheus, arrogance personified.

Why was he thinking of Iván now? He was really off balance.

He gave himself a fast mental shake and forced himself to go back to considering dinner. Even if he didn't go out to eat he should eat fresh food while in port. He retrieved steak, a tomato and lettuce from the refrigerator. A representation of the height of his culinary skill.

Dinner. Then bed?

Or he could wander up to the yacht club and check the noticeboard for deckies. The sooner he found a crew, the sooner he could leave, and suddenly he was eager to leave.

Why had the woman disturbed him? She had nothing to do with him. He didn't need to regard Jenny's refusal as a loss.

'Hello?'

For a moment he thought he was imagining things, but his black mood lifted, just like that, as he abandoned his steak and made his way swiftly up to the deck.

He wasn't imagining things. Jenny was on the jetty, looking almost as he'd last seen her but cleaner. She was still in her battered coat and jeans, but the flour was gone and her curls were damp from washing.

She looked nervous.

'Jenny,' he said and he couldn't disguise the pleasure in his voice. Nor did he want to. Something inside him was very pleased to see her again. *Extremely* pleased.

'I just… I just came out for a walk,' she said.

'Great,' he said.

'Charlie was arrested for drink-driving.'

'Really?'

'That wouldn't have anything to do with you?'

'Who, me?' he demanded, innocence personified. 'Would you like to come on board?'

'I…yes,' she said, and stepped quickly onto the deck as if she was afraid he might rescind his invitation. And suddenly her nerves seemed to be gone. She gazed around in unmistakable awe. 'Wow!'

'Wow' was right. Ramón had no trouble agreeing with Jenny there. *Marquita* was a gracious old lady of the sea, built sixty years ago, a wooden schooner crafted by boat builders who knew their trade and loved what they were doing.

Her hull and cabins were painted white but the timbers of her deck and her trimmings were left unpainted, oiled to a warm honey sheen. Brass fittings glittered in the evening light and, above their heads, *Marquita*'s vast oak masts swayed majestically, matching the faint swell of the incoming tide.

Marquita was a hundred feet of tradition and pure unashamed luxury. Ramón had fallen in love with her the moment he'd seen her, and he watched Jenny's face now and saw exactly the same response.

'What a restoration,' she breathed. 'She's exquisite.'

Now that was different. Almost everyone who saw this boat looked at Ramón and said: 'She must have cost a fortune.'

Jenny wasn't thinking money. She was thinking beauty.

Beauty... There was a word worth lingering on. He watched the delight in Jenny's eyes as she gazed around the deck, taking in every detail, and he thought it wasn't only his boat that was beautiful.

Jenny was almost as golden-skinned as he was; indeed, she could be mistaken for having the same Mediterranean heritage. She was small and compact. Neat, he thought and then thought, no, make that cute. Exceedingly cute. And smart. Her green eyes were bright with intelligence and interest. He thought he was right about the humour as well. She looked like a woman who could smile.

But she wasn't smiling now. She was too awed.

'Can I see below?' she breathed.

'Of course,' he said, and he'd hardly got the words out before she was heading down. He smiled and followed. A man could get jealous. This was one beautiful woman, taking not the slightest interest in him. She was totally entranced by his boat.

He followed her down into the main salon, but was brought up short. She'd stopped on the bottom step, drawing breath, seemingly awed into silence.

He didn't say anything; just waited.

This was the moment for people to gush. In truth, there was much to gush about. The rich oak wainscoting, the burnished timber, the soft worn leather of the deep settees. The wonderful colours and fabrics of the furnishing, the silks and velvets of the cushions and curtains, deep crimsons and dark blues, splashed with touches of bright sunlit gold.

When Ramón had bought this boat, just after the accident that had claimed his mother and sister, she'd been little more than a hull. He'd spent time, care and love on her renovation and his Aunt Sofía had helped as well. In truth, maybe Sofía's additions were a little over the top, but he loved Sofía and he wasn't about to reject her offerings. The result was pure comfort, pure luxury. He loved the *Marquita*—and right now he loved Jenny's reaction.

She was totally entranced, moving slowly around the salon, taking in every detail. This was the main room. The bedrooms were beyond. If she was interested, he'd show her those too, but she wasn't finished here yet.

She prowled, like a small cat inspecting each tiny part of a new territory. Her fingers brushed the burnished timber, lightly, almost reverently. She crossed to the galley and examined the taps, the sink, the stove, the attachments used to hold things steady in a storm. She bent to examine the additional safety features on the stove. Gas stoves on boats could be lethal. Not his. She opened the cupboard below the sink and proceeded to check out the plumbing.

He found he was smiling, enjoying her awe. Enjoying her eye for detail. She glanced up from where she was inspecting the valves below the sink and caught him smiling. And flushed.

'I'm sorry, but it's just so interesting. Is it okay to look?'

'It's more than okay,' he assured her. 'I've never had someone gasp at my plumbing before.'

She didn't return his smile. 'This pump,' she breathed. 'I've seen one in a catalogue. You've got them all through the boat?'

'There are three bathrooms,' he told her, trying not to sound smug. 'All pumped on the same system.'

'You have three bathrooms?' She almost choked. 'My

father didn't hold with plumbing. He said real sailors used buckets. I gather your owner isn't a bucket man.'

'No,' he agreed gravely. 'My owner definitely isn't a bucket man.'

She did smile then, but she was still on the prowl. She crossed to the navigation desk, examining charts, checking the navigation instruments, looking at the radio. Still seeming awed.

Then… 'You leave your radio off?'

'I only use it for outgoing calls.'

'Your owner doesn't mind? With a boat like this, I'd imagine he'd be checking on you daily.'

Your owner…

Now was the time to say he was the owner; this was his boat. But Jenny was starting to relax, becoming companionable, friendly. Ramón had seen enough of other women's reactions when they realised the level of his wealth. For some reason, he didn't want that reaction from Jenny.

Not yet. Not now.

'My owner and I are in accord,' he said gravely. 'We keep in contact when we need to.'

'How lucky,' she said softly. 'To have a boss who doesn't spend his life breathing down your neck.' And then she went right on prowling.

He watched, growing more fascinated by the moment. He'd had boat fanatics on board before—of course he had—and most of them had checked out his equipment with care. Others had commented with envy on the luxury of his fittings and furnishings. But Jenny was seeing the whole thing. She was assessing the boat, and he knew a part of her was also assessing him. In her role as possible hired hand? *Yes*, he thought, starting to feel optimistic. She was now under the impression that his owner trusted him absolutely, and such a reference was obviously doing him no harm.

If he wanted her trust, such a reference was a great way to start.

Finally, she turned back to him, and her awe had been

replaced by a level of satisfaction. As if she'd seen a work of art that had touched a chord deep within. 'I guess now's the time to say, *Isn't she gorgeous*?' she said, and she smiled again. 'Only it's not a question. She just is.'

'I know she is,' he said. He liked her smile. It was just what it should be, lighting her face from within.

She didn't smile enough, he thought.

He thought suddenly of the women he worked with in Bangladesh. Jenny was light years away from their desperate situations, but there was still that shadow behind her smile. As if she'd learned the hard way that she couldn't trust the world.

'Would you like to see the rest of her?' he asked, suddenly unsure where to take this. A tiny niggle was starting in the back of his head. Take this further and there would be trouble…

It was too late. He'd asked. 'Yes, please. Though…it seems an intrusion.'

'It's a pleasure,' he said and he meant it. Then he thought, hey, he'd made his bed this morning. There was a bonus. His cabin practically looked neat.

He took her to the second bedroom first. The cabin where Sofía had really had her way. He'd restored *Marquita* in the months after his mother's and sister's death, and Sofía had poured all her concern into furnishings. 'You spend half your life living on the floor in mud huts in the middle of nowhere,' she'd scolded. 'Your grandmother's money means we're both rich beyond our dreams so there's no reason why you should sleep on the floor here.'

There was certainly no need now for him, or anyone else on this boat, to sleep on the floor. He'd kept a rein on his own room but in this, the second cabin, he'd let Sofía have her way. He opened the door and Jenny stared in stunned amazement— and then burst out laughing.

'It's a boudoir,' she stammered. 'It's harem country.'

'Hey,' he said, struggling to sound serious, even offended, but he found he was smiling as well. Sofía had indeed gone over the top. She'd made a special trip to Marrakesh, and she'd furnished the cabin like a sheikh's boudoir. Boudoir? Who knew? Whatever it was that sheikhs had.

The bed was massive, eight feet round, curtained with burgundy drapes and piled with quilts and pillows of purple and gold. The carpet was thick as grass, a muted pink that fitted beautifully with the furnishings of the bed. Sofía had tied in crisp, pure white linen, and matched the whites with silk hangings of sea scenes on the walls. The glass windows were open while the *Marquita* was in port and the curtains blew softly in the breeze. The room was luxurious, yet totally inviting and utterly, utterly gorgeous.

'This is where you'd sleep,' Ramón told Jenny and she turned and stared at him as if he had two heads.

'Me. The deckie!'

'There are bunkrooms below,' he said. 'But I don't see why we shouldn't be comfortable.'

'This *is* harem country.'

'You don't like it?'

'I love it,' she confessed, eyes huge. 'What's not to love? But, as for sleeping in it… The owner doesn't mind?'

'No.'

'Where do you sleep?' she demanded. 'You can't give me the best cabin.'

'This isn't the best cabin.'

'You're kidding me, right?'

He smiled and led the way back down the companionway. Opened another door. Ushered her in.

He'd decorated this room. Sofía had added a couple of touches—actually, Sofía had spoken to his plumber so the bathroom was a touch…well, a touch embarrassing—but the rest was his.

It was bigger than the stateroom he'd offered Jenny. The bed here was huge but he didn't have hangings. It was more masculine, done in muted tones of the colours through the rest of the boat. The sunlit yellows and golds of the salon had been extended here, with only faint touches of the crimson and blues. The carpet here was blue as well, but short and functional.

There were two amazing paintings on the wall. Recognizable paintings. Jenny gasped with shock. 'Please tell me they're not real.'

Okay. 'They're not real.' They were. 'You want to see the bathroom?' he asked, unable to resist, and he led her through. Then he stood back and grinned as her jaw almost hit the carpet.

While the *Marquita* was being refitted, he'd had to return to Bangladesh before the plumbing was done, and Sofía had decided to put her oar in here as well. And Sofía's oar was not known as sparse and clinical. Plus she had this vision of him in sackcloth and ashes in Bangladesh and she was determined to make the rest of his life what she termed 'comfortable'.

Plus she read romance novels.

He therefore had a massive golden bath in the shape of a Botticelli shell. It stood like a great marble carving in the middle of the room, with carved steps up on either side. Sofía had made concessions to the unsteadiness of bathing at sea by putting what appeared to be vines all around. In reality, they were hand rails but the end result looked like a tableau from the Amazon rainforest. There were gold taps, gold hand rails, splashes of crimson and blue again. *There was trompe l'oeil*—a massive painting that looked like reality—on the wall, making it appear as if the sea came right inside. She'd even added towels with the monogram of the royal family his grandmother had belonged to.

When he'd returned from Bangladesh he'd come in here and nearly had a stroke. His first reaction had been horror, but Sofía had been beside him, so anxious she was quivering.

'I so wanted to give you something special,' she'd said, and Sofía was all the family he had and there was no way he'd hurt her.

He'd hugged her and told her he loved it—and that night he'd even had a bath in the thing. She wasn't to know he usually used the shower down the way.

'You...you sleep in here?' Jenny said, her bottom lip quivering.

'Not in the bath,' he said and grinned.

'But where does the owner sleep?' she demanded, ignoring his attempt at levity. She was gazing around in stupefaction. 'There's not room on his boat for another cabin like this.'

'I... At need I use the bunkroom.' And that was a lie, but suddenly he was starting to really, really want to employ this woman. Okay, he was on morally dubious ground, but did it matter if she thought he was a hired hand? He watched as the strain eased from her face and turned to laughter, and he thought surely this woman deserved a chance at a different life. If one small lie could give it to her...

Would it make a difference if she knew the truth? If he told her he was so rich the offer to pay her debts meant nothing to him... How would she react?

With fear. He'd seen her face when he'd offered her the job. There'd been an intuitive fear that he wanted her for more than her sailing and her cooking. How much worse would it be if she knew he could buy and sell her a thousand times over?

'The owner doesn't mind?' she demanded.

He gave up and went along with it. 'The owner likes his boat to be used and enjoyed.'

'Wow,' she breathed and looked again at the bath. 'Wow!'

'I use the shower in the shared bathroom,' he confessed and she chuckled.

'What a waste.'

'You'd be welcome to use this.'

'In your dreams,' she muttered. 'This place is Harems-R-Us.'

'It's great,' he said. 'But it's still a working boat. I promise you, Jenny, there's not a hint of harem about her.'

'You swear?' she demanded and she fixed him with a look that said she was asking for a guarantee. And he knew what that guarantee was.

'I swear,' he said softly. 'I skipper this boat and she's workmanlike.'

She looked at him for a long, long moment and what she saw finally seemed to satisfy her. She gave a tiny satisfied nod and moved on. 'You have to get her back to Europe fast?'

'Three months, at the latest.' That, at least, was true. His team started work in Bangladesh then and he intended to travel with them. 'So do you want to come?'

'You're still offering?'

'I am.' He ushered her back out of the cabin and closed the door. The sight of that bath didn't make for businesslike discussions on any level.

'You're not employing anyone else?'

'Not if I have you.'

'You don't even know if I can sail,' she said, astounded all over again.

He looked at her appraisingly. The corridor here was narrow and they were too close. He'd like to be able to step back a bit, to see her face. He couldn't.

She was still nervous, he thought, like a deer caught in headlights. But caught she was. His offer seemed to have touched something in her that longed to respond, and even the sight of that crazy bath hadn't made her back off. She was just like he was, he thought, raised with a love of the sea. Aching to be out there.

So…she was caught. All he had to do was reel her in.

'So show me that you can sail,' he said. 'Show me now. The wind's getting up enough to make it interesting. Let's take her out.'

'What, tonight?'

'Tonight. Now. Dare you.'

'I can't,' she said, sounding panicked.

'Why not?'

She stared up at him as if he were a species she'd never seen.

'You just go. Whenever you feel like it.'

'The only thing holding us back is a couple of lines tied to bollards on the wharf,' he said and then, as her look of panic deepened, he grinned. 'But we will bring her back tonight, if that's what's worrying you. It's seven now. We can be back in harbour by midnight.'

'You seriously expect me to sail with you? Now?'

'There's a great moon,' he said. 'The night is ours. Why not?'

So, half an hour later, they were sailing out through the heads, heading for Europe.

Or that was what it felt like to Jenny. Ramón was at the wheel. She'd gone up to the bow to tighten a stay, to see if they could get a bit more tension in the jib. The wind was behind them, the moon was rising from the east, moonlight was shimmering on the water and she was free.

The night was warm enough for her to take off her coat, to put her bare arms out to catch a moonbeam. She could let her hair stream behind her and become a bow-sprite, she thought. An omen of good luck to sailors.

An omen of good luck to Ramón?

She turned and looked back at him. He was a dark shadow in the rear of the boat but she knew he was watching her from behind the wheel. She was being judged?

So what? The boat was as tightly tuned as she could make her. Ramón had asked her to set the sails herself. She'd needed help in this unfamiliar environment but he'd followed her instructions rather than the other way round.

This boat was far bigger than anything she'd sailed on, but she'd spent her life in a sea port, talking to sailors, watching the boats come in. She'd seen yachts like this; she'd watched them and she'd ached to be on one.

She'd brought Matty down to the harbour and she'd promised him his own boat.

'When you're big. When you're strong.'

And suddenly she was blinking back tears. That was stupid. She didn't cry for Matty any more. It was no use; he was never coming back.

'Are you okay?'

Had he seen? The moonlight wasn't that strong. She

swiped her fist angrily across her cheeks, ridding herself of the evidence of her distress, and made her way slowly aft. She had a lifeline clipped to her and she had to clip it and unclip it along the way. She was as sure-footed as a cat at sea, but it didn't hurt to show him she was safety conscious—and, besides, it gave her time to get her face in order.

'I'm fine,' she told him as she reached him.

'Take over the wheel, then,' he told her. 'I need to cook dinner.'

Was this a test, too? she wondered. Did she really have sea legs? Cooking below deck on a heavy swell was something no one with a weak stomach could do.

'I'll do it.' She could.

'You really don't get seasick?'

'I really don't get seasick.'

'A woman in a million,' he murmured and then he grinned. 'But no, it's not fair to ask you to cook. This is your night at sea and, after the day you've had, you deserve it. Take the wheel. Have you eaten?'

'Hours ago.'

'There's steak to spare.' He smiled at her and wham, there it was again, his smile that had her heart saying, *Beware, Beware, Beware*.

'I really am fine,' she said and sat and reached for the wheel and when her hand brushed his—she could swear it was accidental—the *Beware* grew so loud it was a positive roar.

But, seemingly unaware of any roaring on deck, he left her and dropped down into the galley. In minutes the smell of steak wafted up. Nothing else. Just steak.

Not my choice for a lovely night at sea, she thought, but she wasn't complaining. The rolling swell was coming in from the east. She nosed the boat into the swell and the boat steadied on course.

She was the most beautiful boat.

Could she really be crew? She was starting to feel as if, when Ramón had made the offer, she should have signed a contract on the spot. Then, as he emerged from the galley bearing two plates and smiling, she knew why she hadn't. That smile gave her so many misgivings.

'I cooked some for you, too,' he said, looking dubiously down at his plates. 'If you really aren't seasick…'

'I have to eat something to prove it?'

'It's a true test of grit,' he said. 'You eat my cooking, then I know you have a cast iron stomach.' He sat down beside her and handed her a plate.

She looked down at it. Supermarket steak, she thought, and not a good cut.

She poked it with a fork and it didn't give.

'You have to be polite,' he said. 'Otherwise my feelings will be hurt.'

'Get ready for your feelings to be hurt.'

'Taste it at least.'

She released the wheel, fought the steak for a bit and then said, 'Can we put her on automatic pilot? This is going to take some work.'

'Hey, I'm your host,' he said, sounding offended.

'And I'm a cook. How long did you fry this?'

'I don't know. Twenty minutes, maybe? I needed to check the charts to remind myself of the lights for harbour re-entry.'

'So your steak cooked away on its own while you concentrated on other things.'

'What's wrong with that?'

'I'd tell you,' she said darkly, stabbing at her steak and finally managing to saw off a piece. Manfully chewing and then swallowing. 'Only you're right; you're my host.'

'I'd like to be your employer. Will you be cook on the *Marquita*?'

Whoa. So much for concentrating on steak. This, then, was when she had to commit. To craziness or not.

To life—or not.

'You mean…you really were serious with your offer?'

'I'm always serious. It was a serious offer. It *is* a serious offer.'

'You'd only have to pay me a year's salary. I could maybe

organise something…' But she knew she couldn't, and he knew it, too. His response was immediate.

'The offer is to settle your debts and sail away with you, debt free. That or nothing.'

'That sounds like something out of a romance novel. Hero on white charger, rescuing heroine from villain. I'm no wimpy heroine.'

He grinned. 'You sound just like my Aunt Sofía. She reads them, too. But no, I never said you were wimpy. I never thought you were wimpy.'

'I'd repay…'

'No,' he said strongly and took her plate away from her and set it down. He took her hands then, strong hands gripping hers so she felt the strength of him, the sureness and the authority. Authority? This was a man used to getting his own way, she thought, suddenly breathless, and once more came the fleeting thought, *I should run.*

There was nowhere to run. If she said yes there'd be nowhere to run for a year.

'You will not repay,' he growled. 'A deal's a deal, Jenny. You will be my crew. You will be my cook. I'll ask nothing more.'

This was serious. Too serious. She didn't want to think about the implications behind those words.

And maybe she didn't want that promise. *I'll ask nothing more…*

He'd said her debt was insignificant. Maybe it was to him. To her it was an insurmountable burden. She had her pride, but maybe it was time to swallow it, stand aside and let him play hero.

'Thank you,' she said, trying to sound meek.

'Jenny?'

'Yes.'

'I'm captain,' he said. 'But I will not tolerate subordination.'

'Subordination?'

'It's my English,' he apologised, sounding suddenly very Spanish. 'As in captains say to their crew, "*I will not tolerate insubordination!*" just before they give them a hundred lashes and toss them in the brink.'

'What's the brink?'

'I have no idea,' he confessed. 'I'm sure the *Marquita* doesn't have one, which is what I'm telling you. Whereas most captains won't tolerate insubordination, I am the opposite. If you'd like to argue all the way around the Horn, it's fine by me.'

'You want me to argue?' She was too close to him, she thought, and he was still holding her hands. The sensation was worrying.

Worryingly good, though. Not worryingly bad. Arguing with this guy all the way round the Horn...

'Yes. I will also expect muffins,' he said and she almost groaned.

'Really?'

'Take it or leave it,' he said. 'Muffins and insubordination. Yes or no?'

She stared up at him in the moonlight. He stared straight back at her and she felt her heart do this strange surge, as if her fuel-lines had just been doubled.

What am I getting into, she demanded of herself, but suddenly she didn't care. The night was warm, the boat was lovely and this man was holding her hands, looking down at her in the moonlight and his hands were imparting strength and sureness and promise.

Promise? What was he promising? She was being fanciful.

But she had to be careful, she told herself fiercely. She must.

It was too late.

'Yes,' she said before she could change her mind—and she was committed.

She was heading to the other side of the world with a man she'd met less than a day ago.

Was she out of her mind?

* * *

What had he done? What was he getting himself into?

He'd be spending three months at sea with a woman called Jenny.

Jenny what? Jenny who? He knew nothing about her other than she sailed and she cooked.

He spent more time on background checks for the deckies he employed. He always ran a fast check on the kids he employed, to ensure there weren't skeletons in the closet that would come bursting out the minute he was out of sight of land.

And he didn't employ them for a year. The deal was always that they'd work for him until the next port and then make a mutual decision as to whether they wanted to go on.

He'd employed Jenny for a year.

He wasn't going to be on the boat for a year. Had he thought that through? No, so he'd better think it through now.

Be honest? Should he say, *Jenny, I made the offer because I felt sorry for you, and there was no way you'd have accepted my offer of a loan if you knew I'm only offering three months' work?*

He wasn't going to say that, because it wasn't true. He'd made the offer for far more complicated reasons than sympathy, and that was what was messing with his head now.

In three months he'd be in Bangladesh.

Did he need to go to Bangladesh?

In truth, he didn't need to go anywhere. His family inheritance had been massive, he'd invested it with care and if he wished he could spend the rest of his life in idle luxury.

Only…his family had never been like that. Excluded from the royal family, Ramón's grandmother had set about making herself useful. The royal family of Cepheus was known for indolence, mindless indulgence, even cruelty. His grandmother had left the royal palace in fear, for good reason. But then she'd started making herself a life—giving life to others.

So she and her children, Ramón's father and aunt, had set up a charity in Bangladesh. They built homes in the low lying delta regions, houses that could be raised as flood levels rose, homes that could keep a community safe and dry. Ramón had been introduced to it early and found the concept fascinating.

His father's death had made him even more determined to stay away from royalty; to make a useful life for himself, so at seventeen he'd apprenticed himself to one of Cepheus's top builders. He'd learned skills from the ground up. Now it wasn't just money he was throwing at this project—it was his hands as well as his heart.

During the wet season he couldn't build. During these months he used to stay on the island he still called home, spending time with his mother and sister. He'd also spent it planning investments so the work they were doing could go on for ever.

But then his mother and his sister died. One drunken driver and his family was wiped out. Suddenly he couldn't bear to go home. He employed a team of top people to take over his family's financial empire, and he'd bought the *Marquita*.

He still worked in Bangladesh—hands-on was great, hard manual work which drove away the demons. But for the rest of the year he pitted himself against the sea and felt better for it.

But there was a gaping hole where his family had been; a hole he could never fill. Nor did he want to, he decided after a year or so. If it hurt so much to lose…to get close to someone again seemed stupid.

So why ask Jenny onto his boat? He knew instinctively that closeness was a very real risk with this woman. But it was as if another part of him, a part he didn't know existed, had emerged and done the asking.

He'd have to explain Bangladesh to her. Or would he? When he got to Cepheus he could simply say there was no need for the boat, the owner wanted her in dry dock for six months. Jenny was free to fly back to Australia—he'd pay her fare—and she could fill the rest of her contract six months later.

That'd mean he had crew not only for now but for the future as well.

A crew of one woman.

This was danger territory. The Ramón he knew well, the Ramón he trusted, was screaming a warning.

No. He could be sensible. This was a big enough boat for him to keep his own counsel. He'd learned to do that from years of sailing with deckies. The kids found him aloof, he knew, but aloof was good. Aloof meant you didn't open yourself to gut-wrenching pain.

Aloof meant you didn't invite a woman like Jenny to sail around the world with you.

A shame that he just had.

'The *Marquita*'s reported as having left Fiji two weeks ago. We think Ramón's in Australia.'

'For heaven's sake!' Sofía pushed herself up on her cushions and stared at the lawyer, perplexed. 'What's he doing in Australia?'

'Who would know?' the lawyer said with asperity. 'He's left no travel plans.'

'He could hardly expect this awfulness,' Sofía retorted. 'There's never been a thought that Ramón could inherit.'

'Well, it makes life difficult for us,' the lawyer snapped. 'He doesn't even answer incoming radio calls.'

'Ramón's been a loner since his mother and sister died,' Sofía said, and she sighed. 'It affected me deeply, so who knows how it affected him? If he wants to be alone, who are we to stop him?'

'He can't be alone any longer,' the lawyer said. 'I'm flying out.'

'To Australia?'

'Yes.'

'Isn't Australia rather big?' Sofía said cautiously. 'I mean... I don't want to discourage you, but if you flew to Perth and he ended up at Darwin... I've read about Australia and it does sound a little larger than Cepheus.'

'I believe the smallest of its states is bigger than Cepheus,' the lawyer agreed. 'But if he's coming from Fiji he'll be heading for the east coast. We have people looking out for him at every major port. If I wait in Sydney I can be with him in hours rather than days.'

'You don't think we could wait until he makes contact?' Sofía said. 'He does email me. Eventually.'

'He needs to take the throne by the end of the month or Carlos inherits.'

'Carlos?' Sofía said, and her face crumpled in distress. 'Oh, dear.'

'So you see the hurry,' the lawyer said. 'If I'm in Australia, as soon as we locate his boat I can be there. He has to come home. Now.'

'I wish we could find him before I make a decision about Philippe,' she said. 'Oh, dear.'

'I thought you'd found foster parents for him.'

'Yes, but…it seems wrong to send him away from the palace. What would Ramón do, do you think?'

'I hardly think Prince Ramón will wish to be bothered with a child.'

'No,' Sofía said sadly. 'Maybe you're right. There are so many things Ramón will be bothered with now—how can he want a say in the future of a child he doesn't know?'

'He won't. Send the child to foster parents.'

'Yes,' Sofía said sadly. 'I don't know how to raise a child myself. He's had enough of hired nannies. I think it's best for everyone.'

CHAPTER THREE

THIS was really, really foolish. She was allowing an unknown Spaniard to pay her debts and sweep her off in his fabulous yacht to the other side of the world. She was so appalled at herself she couldn't stop grinning.

Watching Cathy's face had been a highlight. 'I can't let you do it,' she'd said in horror. 'I know I joked about it but I never dreamed you'd take me seriously. You know nothing about him. This is awful.'

And Jenny had nodded solemn agreement.

'It is awful. If I turn up in some Arabic harem on the other side of the world it's all your fault,' she told her friend. 'You pointed him out to me.'

'No. Jenny, I never would have... No!'

She'd chuckled and relented. 'Okay, I won't make you come and rescue me. I know this is a risk, my love, but honestly, he seems nice. I don't think there's a harem but even if there is...I'm a big girl and I take responsibility for my own decision. I know it's playing with fire, but honestly, Cathy, you were right. I'm out of here any way I can.'

And what a way! Sailing out of the harbour on board the *Marquita* with Ramón at the helm was like something out of a fairy tale.

Fairy tales didn't include scrubbing decks, though, she conceded ruefully. There was enough of reality to keep her grounded—or as grounded as one could be at sea. Six days later, Jenny was on her knees swishing a scrubbing brush like a true deck-hand. They'd been visited by a flock of terns at dawn—possibly the last they'd see until they neared land again. She certainly hoped so. The deck was a mess.

But making her feel a whole lot better about scrubbing was the fact that Ramón was on his knees scrubbing as well. That didn't fit the fairy tale either. Knight on white charger scrubbing bird droppings? She glanced over and found he was watching her. He caught her grin and he grinned back.

'Not exactly the romantic ideal of sailing into the sunset,' he said, and it was so much what she'd been thinking that she laughed. She sat back on her heels, put her face up to the sun and soaked it in. The *Marquita* was on autopilot, safe enough in weather like this. There was a light breeze—enough to make *Marquita* slip gracefully through the water like a skier on a downhill run. On land it would be hot, but out here on the ocean it was just plain fabulous. Jenny was wearing shorts and T-shirt and nothing else. Her feet were bare, her hair was scrunched up in a ponytail to keep it out of her eyes, her nose was white with sunscreen—and she was perfectly, gloriously happy.

'You're supposed to complain,' Ramón said, watching her. 'Any deckie I've ever employed would be complaining by now.'

'What on earth would I be complaining about?'

'Scrubbing, maybe?'

'I'd scrub from here to China if I could stay on this boat,' she said happily and then saw his expression and hastily changed her mind. 'No. I didn't mean that. You keep right on thinking I'm working hard for my money. But, honestly, you have the best job in the world, Ramón Cavellero, and I have the second best.'

'I do, don't I?' he said, but his smile faded, and something about him said he had shadows too. Did she want to ask?

Maybe not.

She'd known Ramón for over a week now, and she'd learned a lot in that time. She'd learned he was a wonderful sailor, intuitive, clever and careful. He took no unnecessary risks, yet on the second night out there'd been a storm. A nervous sailor might have reefed in everything and sat it out. Ramón, however, had looked at the charts, altered his course and let the jib stay at full stretch. The *Marquita* had flown across the water with a speed Jenny found unbelievable, and when the dawn came and the storm abated they were maybe three hundred miles further towards New Zealand than they'd otherwise have been.

She'd taken a turn at the wheel that night but she knew Ramón hadn't slept. She'd been conscious of his shadowy presence below, aware of what the boat was doing, aware of how she was handling her. It wasn't that he didn't trust her, but she was new crew and to sleep in such a storm while she had such responsibility might have been dangerous.

His competence pleased her, as did the fact that he hadn't told her he was checking on her. Lots of things about him pleased her, she admitted—but Ramón kept himself to himself. Any thoughts she may have had of being an addition to his harem were quickly squashed. Once they were at sea, he was reserved to the point of being aloof.

'How long have you skippered this boat?' she asked suddenly, getting back to scrubbing, not looking up. She was learning that he responded better that way, talking easily as they worked together. Once work stopped he retreated again into silence.

'Ten years,' he said.

'Wow. You must have been at kindergarten when you were first employed.'

'I got lucky,' he said brusquely, and she thought, *don't go there*. She'd asked a couple of things about the owner, and she'd learned quickly that was the way to stop a conversation dead.

'So how many crews would you have employed in that time?' she asked. And then she frowned down at what she was scrubbing. How on earth had the birds managed to soil under the rim of the forward hatch? She tried to imagine, and couldn't.

'How long's a piece of string?' Ramón said. 'I get new people at every port.'

'But you have me for a year.'

'That's right, I have,' he said and she glanced up and caught a flash of something that might be satisfaction. She smiled and went back to scrubbing, unaccountably pleased.

'That sounds like you liked my lunch time paella.'

'I loved your lunch time paella. Where did you learn to cook something so magnificently Spanish?'

'I'm part Spanish,' she said and he stopped scrubbing and stared.

'Spanish?'

'Well, truthfully, I'm all Australian,' she said, 'but my father was Spanish. He moved to Australia when he met my mother. My mother's mother was Spanish as well. Papà came as an adventuring young man. He contacted my grandmother as a family friend and the rest is history.

'So,' Ramón said slowly, sounding dazed. '*Habla usted español?* Can you speak Spanish?'

'*Sí*,' she said, and tried not to sound smug.

'I don't believe it.'

'There's no end to my talents,' she agreed and grinned, and then peered under the hatch. 'Speaking of talent… How did these birds do this? They must have lain on their sides and aimed.'

'It's a competition between them and me,' Ramón said darkly. 'They don't like my boat looking beautiful. All I can do is sail so far out to sea they can't reach me. But…you have a Spanish background? Why didn't you tell me?'

'You never asked,' she said, and then she hesitated. 'There's lots you didn't ask, and your offer seemed so amazing I saw no reason to mess it with detail. I could have told you I play a mean game of netball, I can climb trees, I have my bronze surf lifesaving certificate and I can play *Waltzing Matilda* on a gum leaf. You didn't ask and how could I tell you? You might have thought I was skiting.'

'Skiting?'

'Making myself out to be Miss Wonderful.'

'I seem to have employed Miss Wonderful regardless,' he said. And then... 'Jenny?'

'Mmm?'

'No, I mean, what sort of Spanish parents call their daughter Jenny?'

'It's Gianetta.'

'Gianetta.' He said it with slow, lilting pleasure, and he said it the way it was supposed to sound. The way her parents had said it. She blinked and then she thought no. Actually, the way Ramón said it wasn't the way her parents had said it. He had the pronunciation right but it was much, much better. He rolled it, he almost growled it, and it sounded so sexy her toes started to curl.

'I would have found out when you signed your contract,' Ramón was saying while she attempted a bit of toe uncurling. Then he smiled. 'Speaking of which, maybe it's time you did sign up. I don't want to let anyone who can play *Waltzing Matilda* on a gum leaf get away.'

'It's a dying art,' she said, relieved to be on safer ground. In fact she'd been astounded that he hadn't yet got round to making her sign any agreement.

The day before they'd sailed he'd handed Charlie a cheque. 'How do you know you can trust me to fill my part of the bargain?' she'd asked him, stunned by what he was doing, and Ramón had looked down at her for a long moment, his face impassive, and he'd given a small decisive nod.

'I can,' he'd said, and that was that.

'Playing a gum leaf's a dying art?' he asked now, cautiously.

'It's something I need to teach my grandchildren,' she told him. And then she heard what she'd said. *Grandchildren*. The void, always threatening, was suddenly right under her. She hauled herself back with an effort.

'What is it?' Ramón said and he was looking at her with concern. The void disappeared. There went her toes again, curling, curling. Did he have any idea of what those eyes did to her? They helped, though. She was back again now, safe. She could move on. If she could focus on something other than those eyes.

'So I'm assuming you're Spanish, too?' she managed.

'No!'

'You're not Spanish?'

'Absolutely not.'

'You sound Spanish.' Then she hesitated. Here was another reason she hadn't told him about her heritage—she wasn't sure. There was something else in his accent besides Spain. France? It was a sexy mix that she couldn't quite place.

'I come from Cepheus,' he said, and all was explained. Cepheus. She knew it. A tiny principality on the Mediterranean, fiercely independent and fiercely proud.

'My father told me about Cepheus,' she said, awed that here was an echo from her childhood. 'Papà was born not so far away from the border and he went there as a boy. He said it's the most beautiful country in the world—but he also said it belonged to Spain.'

'If he's Spanish then he would say that,' Ramón growled. 'If he was French he'd say the same thing. They've been fighting over my country for generations, like eagles over a small bird. What they've come to realize, however, is that the small bird has claws and knows how to protect itself. For now they've dropped us—they've let us be. We are Cepheus. Nothing more.'

'But you speak Spanish?'

'The French and the Spanish have both taken part of our language and made it theirs,' he said, and she couldn't help herself. She chuckled.

'What's funny?' He was suddenly practically glowering.

'Your patriotism,' she said, refusing to be deflected. 'Like Australians saying the English speak Australian with a plum in their mouths.'

'It's not the same,' he said but then he was smiling again. She smiled back—and wham.

What was it with this man?

She knew exactly what it was. Quite simply he was the most gorgeous guy she'd ever met. Tall, dark and fabulous, a voice like a god, rugged, clever…and smiling. She took a deep breath and went back to really focused scrubbing. It was imperative that she scrub.

She was alone on a boat in the middle of the ocean with a man she was so attracted to her toes were practically ringlets. And she was crew. Nothing more. She was cook and deckhand. Remember it!

'So why the debt?' he asked gently, and she forgot about being cook and deckhand. He was asking as if he cared.

Should she tell him to mind his own business? Should she back away?

Why? He'd been extraordinarily kind and if he wanted to ask… He didn't feel like her boss, and at this moment she didn't feel like a deckie.

Maybe he even had the right to know.

'I lost my baby,' she said flatly, trying to make it sound as if it was history. Only of course she couldn't. Two years on, it still pierced something inside her to say it. 'Matty was born with a congenital heart condition. He had a series of operations, each riskier than the last. Finally, there was only one procedure left to try—a procedure so new it cost the earth. It was his last chance and I had to take it, but of course I'd run out of what money I had. I was working for Charlie for four hours a day over the lunch time rush—Matty was in hospital and I hated leaving him but I had to pay the rent, so when things hit rock bottom Charlie knew. So Charlie loaned me what I needed on the basis that I keep working on for him.'

She scrubbed fiercely at a piece of deck that had already been scrubbed. Ramón didn't say anything. She scrubbed a bit more. Thought about not saying more and then decided— why not say it all?

'You need to understand…I'd been cooking on the docks

since I was seventeen and people knew my food. Charlie's café was struggling and he needed my help to keep it afloat. But the operation didn't work. Matty died when he was two years, three months and five days old. I buried him and I went back to Charlie's café and I've been there ever since.'

'I am so sorry.' Ramón was sitting back on his heels and watching her. She didn't look up—she couldn't. She kept right on scrubbing.

The boat rocked gently on the swell. The sun shone down on the back of her neck and she was acutely aware of his gaze. So aware of his silence.

'Charlie demanded that you leave your baby, for those hours in the last days of his life?' he said at last, and she swallowed at that, fighting back regret that could never fade.

'It was our deal.' She hesitated. 'You've seen the worst of Charlie. Time was when he was a decent human being. Before the drink took over. When he offered me a way out—I only saw the money. I guess I just trusted. And after I borrowed the money there was no way out.'

'So where,' he asked, in his soft, lilting accent that seemed to have warmth and sincerity built into it, 'was Matty's father?'

'On the other side of the world, as far as I know,' she said, and she blinked back self-pity and found herself smiling. 'My Kieran. Or, rather, no one's Kieran.'

'You're smiling?' He sounded incredulous, as well he might.

'Yes, that's stupid. And yes, I was really stupid.' Enough with the scrubbing—any more and she'd start taking off wood. She tossed her brush into the bucket and stood up, leaning against the rail and letting the sun comfort her. How to explain Kieran? 'My father had just died, and I was bleak and miserable. Kieran came into port and he was just…alive. I met him on the wharf one night, we went dancing and I fell in love. Only even then I knew I wasn't in love with Kieran. Not with the person. I was in love with what he represented. Happiness. Laughter. Life. At the end of a wonderful week he sailed away and two weeks later I discovered our precautions hadn't worked. I emailed him to tell him. He sent me a dozen roses and a cheque for a termination. The next time I emailed, to tell him I was keeping our baby, there was no reply. There's been no reply since.'

'Do you mind?' he said gently.

'I mind that Kieran didn't have a chance to meet his son,' she said. 'It was his loss. Matty was wonderful.' She pulled herself together and managed to smile again. 'But I'd imagine all mothers say that about their babies. Any minute now I'll be tugging photographs out of my purse.'

'It would be my privilege to see them.'

'You don't mean that.'

'Why would I not?'

Her smile faded. She searched his face and saw only truth.

'It's okay,' she said, disconcerted. She was struggling to understand this man. She'd accepted this job suspecting he was another similar to Kieran, sailing the world to escape responsibility, only the more she saw of him the more she realized there were depths she couldn't fathom.

She had armour now to protect herself against the likes of Kieran. She knew she did—that was why she'd taken the job. But this man's gentle sympathy and practical help were something new. She tried to imagine Kieran scrubbing a deck when he didn't have to, and she couldn't.

'So where's your family?' she asked, too abruptly, and she watched his face close. Which was what she was coming to expect. He'd done this before to her, simply shutting himself off from her questions. She thought it was a method he'd learned from years of employing casual labour, setting boundaries and staying firmly behind them.

Maybe that was reasonable, she conceded. Just because she'd stepped outside her personal boundaries, it didn't mean he must.

'Sorry. I'll put the buckets away,' she said, but he didn't move and neither did she.

'I don't like talking of my family.'

'That's okay. That's your right.'

'You didn't have to tell me about your son.'

'Yes, but I like talking about Matty,' she said. She thought about it. It wasn't absolutely true. Or was it?

She only talked about Matty to Cathy, to Susie, to those few people who'd known him. But still…

'Talking about him keeps him real,' she said, trying to figure it out as she spoke. 'Keeping silent locks him in my heart and I'm scared he'll shrivel. I want to be able to have him out there, to share him.' She shrugged. 'It makes no sense but there it is. Your family…you keep them where you need to have them. I'm sorry I intruded.'

'I don't believe you could ever intrude,' he said, so softly she could hardly hear him. 'But my story's not so peaceful. My father died when I was seven. He and my grandfather… well, let's just say they didn't get on. My grandfather was what might fairly be described as a wealthy thug. He mistreated my grandmother appallingly, and finally my father thought to put things right by instigating legal proceedings. Only when it looked like my father and grandmother might win, my grandfather's thugs bashed him—so badly he died.'

'Oh, Ramón,' she whispered, appalled.

'It's old history,' he said in a voice that told her it wasn't. It still had the power to hurt. 'Nothing could ever be proved, so we had to move on as best we could. But my grandmother never got over it. She died when I was ten, and then my mother and my sister were killed in a car accident when I was little more than a teenager. So that's my family. Or, rather, that was my family. I have an aunt I love, but that's all.'

'So you don't have a home,' she said softly.

'The sea makes a wonderful mistress.'

'She's not exactly cuddly,' Jenny retorted before she thought it through, and then she heard what she'd said and she could have kicked herself. But it seemed her tongue was determined to keep her in trouble. 'I mean… Well, the sea. A *mistress*? Wouldn't you rather have a real one?'

His lips twitched. 'You're asking why don't I have a woman?'

'I didn't mean that at all,' she said, astounded at herself. 'If you don't choose to…'

But she stopped herself there. She was getting into deeper water at every word and she was floundering.

'Would you rate yourself as cuddly?' he asked, a slight smile still playing round his mouth, and she felt herself colouring from the toes up. She'd walked straight into that one.

He thoroughly disconcerted her. It was as if there was some sort of connection between them, like an electric current that buzzed back and forth, no matter how she tried to subdue it.

She had to subdue it. Ramón was her boss. She had to maintain a working relationship with him for a year.

'No. No!' She shook her head so hard the tie came loose and her curls went flying every which way. 'Of course I'm not cuddly. I got myself in one horrible mess with Kieran, and I'm not going down that path again, thank you very much.'

'So maybe the sea is to be your partner in life, too?'

'I don't want a partner,' she said with asperity. 'I don't need one, thank you very much. You're very welcome to your sea, Mr Cavellero, but I'll stick to cooking, sailing and occasional scrubbing. What more could a woman want? It sounds like relationships, for both of us, are a thing of the past.' And then she paused. She stared out over Ramón's shoulder. 'Oh!' She put her hand up to shade her eyes. 'Oh, Ramón, look!'

Ramón wheeled to see what she was seeing, and he echoed her gasp.

They'd been too intent on each other to notice their surroundings—the sea was clear to the horizon so there was no threat, but suddenly there was a great black mound, floating closer and closer to the *Marquita*. On the far side of the mound was another, much smaller.

The smaller mound was gliding through the water, surfacing and diving, surfacing and diving. The big mound lay still, like a massive log, three-quarters submerged.

'Oh,' Jenny gasped, trying to take in what she was seeing. 'It's a whale and its calf. But why...'

Why was the larger whale so still?

They were both staring out to starboard now. Ramón narrowed his eyes, then swore and made his way swiftly aft. He retrieved a pair of field glasses, focused and swore again.

'She's wrapped in a net.' He flicked off the autopilot. 'Jenny, we're coming about.'

The boat was already swinging. Jenny dropped her buckets and moved like lightning, reefing in the main with desperate haste so the boom wouldn't slam across with the wind shift.

Even her father wouldn't have trusted her to move so fast, she thought, as she winched in the stays with a speed even she hadn't known was possible. Ramón expected the best of her and she gave it.

But Ramón wasn't focused on her. All his attention was on the whale. With the sails in place she could look again at what was in front of her. And what she saw... She drew in her breath in distress.

The massive whale—maybe fifty feet long or more—was almost completely wrapped in a damaged shark net. Jenny had seen these nets. They were set up across popular beaches to keep swimmers safe, but occasionally whales swam in too close to shore and became entangled, or swam into a net that had already been dislodged.

The net was enfolding her almost completely, with a rope as thick as Jenny's wrist tying her from head to tail, forcing her to bend. As the *Marquita* glided past, Jenny saw her massive pectoral fins were fastened uselessly to her sides. She was rolling helplessly in the swell.

Dead?

No. Just as she thought it, the creature gave a massive shudder. She was totally helpless, and by her side her calf swam free, but helpless as well in the shadow of her mother's entrapment.

'*Dios*,' she whispered. It was the age-old plea she'd learned from her mother, and she heard the echo of it from Ramón's lips.

'It's a humpback,' she said in distress. 'The net's wrapped so tight it's killing her. What can we do?'

But Ramón was already moving. 'We get the sails down and start the motor,' he said. 'The sails won't give us room to manoeuvre. Gianetta, I need your help. Fast.'

He had it. The sails were being reefed in almost before he finished speaking, as the motor hummed seamlessly into life.

He pushed it into low gear so the sound was a low hum. The last thing either of them wanted was to panic the whale. As it was, the calf was moving nervously away from them, so the mother was between it and the boat.

'If she panics there's nothing we can do,' Jenny said grimly. 'Can we get near enough to cut?'

They couldn't. Ramón edged the *Marquita* close, the big whale rolled a little, the swell separated them and Jenny knew they could never simply reach out and cut.

'Can we call someone?' she said helplessly. 'There's whale rescue organisations. Maybe they could come out.'

'We're too far from land,' Ramón said. 'It's us or no one.'

No one, Jenny thought as they tried one more pass. It was hopeless. For them to cut the net the whale had to be right beside the boat. With the lurching of the swell there was no way they could steer the boat alongside and keep her there.

How else to help? To get into the water and swim, then cling and cut was far, far too risky. Jenny was a good swimmer but…

'It's open water, the job's too big, there's no way I could count on getting back into the boat,' Ramón said, and she knew he was thinking the same.

'You would do it if you could?' she asked, incredulous.

'If I knew it'd be effective. But do you think she's going to stay still while I cut? If she rolled, if I was pushed under and caught…'

As if on cue, the whale rolled again. Her massive pectoral fins were fastened hard against her, so a sideways roll was all she could do. She blew—a spray of water misted over Jenny's face, but Jenny's face was wet anyway.

'We can't leave her like this,' she whispered. 'We have to try.'

'We do,' Ramón said. 'Jenny, are you prepared to take a risk?'

There was no question. 'Of course.'

'Okay,' he said, reaching under the seat near the wheel and hauling out life jackets. 'Here's the plan. We put these on. We unfasten the life raft in case worst comes to worst and we let the authorities know what's happening. We radio in our position, we tell them what we intend to do and if they don't hear back from us then they'll know we're sitting in a life raft in the middle of the Pacific. We're wearing positional locators anyway. We should be fine.'

'What…what are we intending to do?' Jenny asked faintly.

'Pull the boat up beside the whale,' he said. 'If you're brave enough.'

She stared at him, almost speechless. How could he get so close? And, even if he did, if the whale rolled… 'You'd risk the boat?' she gasped.

'Yes.' Unequivocal.

'Could we be sure of rescue?'

'I'll set it up so we would be,' he said. 'I'm not risking our lives here. Only our boat and the cost of marine rescue.'

'Marine rescue… It'd cost a fortune.'

'Jenny, we're wasting time. Yes or no?'

She looked out at the whale. Left alone, she'd die, dreadfully, agonisingly and, without her, her calf would slowly starve to death as well.

Ramón was asking her to risk all. She looked at him and he met her gaze, levelly and calmly.

'Gianetta, she's helpless,' he said. 'I believe at some subliminal level she'll understand we're trying to help and she won't roll towards us. But you know I can't guarantee that. There's a small chance we may end up sitting in a lifeboat for the next few hours waiting to be winched to safety. But I won't do it unless I have your agreement. It's not my risk, Gianetta. It's our risk.'

Our risk.

She thought about what he was asking—what he was doing. He'd have to explain to his owner that he'd lost his boat to save a whale. He'd lose his job at the very least. Maybe he'd be up for massive costs, for the boat and for rescue.

She looked at him and she saw it meant nothing.

He was free, she thought, with a sudden stab of something that could almost be jealousy. There was the whale to be saved. He'd do what needed to be done without thinking of the future.

Life… That was all that mattered, she thought suddenly, and with it came an unexpected lifting of the dreariness of the last couple of years. She'd fought long and hard for Matty. She'd lost but she'd had him and she'd loved him and she'd worried about the cost later.

She looked out at the whale and she knew there was only one answer to give.

'Of course,' she said. 'Just give me a couple of minutes to stick a ration pack in the life raft. If I'm going to float around for a day or so waiting for rescue flights then I want at least two bottles of champagne and some really good cheeses while I'm waiting.'

Jenny didn't have a clue what Ramón intended, but when she saw she was awed. With his safeguards in place, he stood on the highest point of the boat with a small anchor—one he presumably used in shallow waters when lowering the massive main anchor would potentially damage the sea bed.

This anchor was light enough for a man to hold. Or, rather, for Ramón to hold, Jenny corrected herself. It still looked heavy. But Ramón stood with the anchor attached by a long line and he held it as if it was no weight at all, while Jenny nosed the boat as close to the whale as she dared. Ramón swung the anchor round and round, in wider and wider circles, and then he heaved with every ounce of strength he had.

The whale was maybe fifteen feet from the boat. The anchor flew over the far side of her and slid down. As it slid,

Ramón was already striding aft, a far more secure place to manoeuvre, and he was starting to tug the rope back in.

'Cut the motor,' he snapped. She did, and finally she realized what he was doing.

The anchor had fallen on the far side of the whale. As Ramón tugged, the anchor was being hauled up the whale's far side. Its hooks caught the ropes of the net and held, and suddenly Ramón was reeling in the anchor with whale attached. Or, rather, the *Marquita* was being reeled in against the whale, and the massive creature was simply submitting.

Jenny was by Ramón's side in an instant, pulling with him. Boat and whale moved closer. Closer still.

'Okay, hold her as close as you can,' Ramón said curtly as the whale's vast body came finally within an arm's length. 'If she pulls, you let go. No heroics, Gianetta, just do it. But keep tension on the rope so I'll know as soon as I have it free.'

Ramón had a lifeline clipped on. He was leaning over the side, with a massive gutting knife in his hand. Reaching so far Jenny was sure he'd fall.

The whale could roll this way, she thought wildly, and if she did he could be crushed. He was supporting himself on the whale itself, his legs still on the boat, but leaning so far over he was holding onto the netting. Slicing. Slicing. As if the danger was nothing.

She tugged on. If the whale pulled away, she'd have to release her. They'd lose the anchor. They had this one chance. Please...

But the whale didn't move, except for the steady rise and fall of the swell, where Jenny had to let out, reel in, let out, reel in, to try and keep Ramón's base steady against her.

He was slicing and slicing and slicing, swearing and slicing some more, until suddenly the tension on Jenny's rope was no longer there. The anchor lifted free, the net around the whale's midriff dislodged. Jenny, still pulling, was suddenly reeling in a mass of netting and an anchor.

And Ramón was back in the boat, pulling with her.

One of the whale's fins was free. The whale moved it a

little, stretching, and she floated away. Not far. Twenty feet, no more.

The whale stilled again. One fin was not enough. She was still trapped.

On the far side of her, her calf nudged closer.

'Again,' Ramón said grimly as Jenny gunned the motor back into action and nosed close. He was already on top of the cabin, swinging the anchor rope once more. 'If she'll let us.'

'You'll hit the calf,' she said, almost to herself, and then bit her tongue. Of all the stupid objections. She knew what his answer must be.

'It's risk the calf having a headache, or both of them dying. No choice.'

But he didn't need to risk. As the arcs of the swinging anchor grew longer, the calf moved away again.

As if it knew.

And, once again, Ramón caught the net.

It took an hour, maybe longer, the times to catch the net getting longer as the amount of net left to cut off grew smaller. But they worked on, reeling her in, slicing, reeling her in, slicing, until the netting was a massive pile of rubbish on the deck.

Ramón was saving her, Jenny thought dazedly as she worked on. Every time he leaned out he was risking his life. She watched him work—and she fell in love.

She was magnificent. Ramón was working feverishly, slashing at the net while holding on to the rails and stretching as far as he could, but every moment he did he was aware of Jenny.

Gianetta.

She had total control of the anchor rope, somehow holding the massive whale against the side of the boat. But they both knew that to hold the boat in a fixed hold would almost certainly mean capsizing. What Jenny had to do was to work with the swells, holding the rope fast, then loosening it as the whale rose and the boat swayed, or the whale sank and the boat rose. Ramón had no room for anything but holding on to the boat and slashing but, thanks to Jenny, he had an almost stable platform to work with.

Tied together, boat and whale represented tonnage he didn't want to think about, especially as he was risking slipping between the two.

He wouldn't slip. Jenny was playing her part, reading the sea, watching the swell, focused on the whale in case she suddenly decided to roll or pull away...

She didn't. Ramón could slash at will at the rope entrapment, knowing Jenny was keeping him safe.

He slipped once and he heard her gasp. He felt her hand grip his ankle.

He righted himself—it was okay—but the memory of her touch stayed.

Gianetta was watching out for him.

Gianetta. Where had she come from, this magical Gianetta?

It was working. Jenny was scarcely breathing. Please, please...

But somehow her prayers were being answered. Piece by piece the net was being cut away. Ramón was winning. They were both winning.

The last section to be removed was the netting and the ropes trapping and tying the massive tail, but catching this section was the hardest. Ramón threw and threw, but each time the anchor slipped uselessly behind the whale and into the sea.

To have come so far and not save her... Jenny felt sick.

But Ramón would not give up. His arm must be dropping off, she thought, but just as she reached the point where despair took over, the whale rolled. She stretched and lifted her tail as far as she could within the confines of the net, and in doing so she made a channel to trap the anchor line as Ramón threw. And her massive body edged closer to the boat.

Ramón threw again, and this time the anchor held.

Once more Jenny reeled her in and once more Ramón sliced. Again. Again. One last slash—and the last piece of rope came loose into his hands.

Ramón staggered back onto the deck and Jenny was hauling the anchor in one last time. He helped her reel it in, then they stood together in the mass of tangled netting on the deck, silent, awed, stunned, as the whale finally floated free. Totally free. The net was gone.

But there were still questions. Were they too late? Had she been trapped too long?

Ramón's arm came round Jenny's waist and held, but Jenny was hardly aware of it. Or maybe she was, but it was all part of this moment. She was breathing a plea and she knew the plea was echoing in Ramón's heart as well as her own.

Please…

The whale was wallowing in the swell, rolling up and down, up and down. Her massive pectoral fins were free now. They moved stiffly outward, upward, over and over, while Jenny and Ramón held their breath and prayed.

The big tail swung lazily back and forth; she seemed to be stretching, feeling her freedom. Making sure the ropes were no longer there.

'She can't have been caught all that long,' Jenny whispered, breathless with wonder. 'Look at her tail. That rope was tied so tightly but there's hardly a cut.'

'She might have only just swum into it,' Ramón said and Jenny was aware that her awe was echoed in his voice. His arm had tightened around her and it seemed entirely natural. This was a prayer shared. 'If it was loosened from the shore by a storm it might have only hit her a day or so ago. The calf looks healthy enough.'

The calf was back at its mother's side now, nudging against her flank. Then it dived, straight down into the deep, and Jenny managed a faltering smile.

'He'll be feeding. She must still have milk. Oh, Ramón…'

'Gianetta,' Ramón murmured back, and she knew he was feeling exactly what she was feeling. Awe, hope, wonder. They might, they just might, have been incredibly, wondrously lucky.

And then the big whale moved. Her body seemed to ripple. Everything flexed at once, her tail, her fins... She rolled away, almost onto her back, as if to say to her calf: *No feeding, not yet, I need to figure if I'm okay.*

And figure she did. She swam forward in front of the boat, speeding up, speeding up. Faster, faster she swam, with her calf speeding after her.

And then, just as they thought they'd lost sight of her, she came sweeping back, a vast majestic mass of glossy black muscle and strength and bulk. Then, not a hundred yards from the boat, she rolled again, only higher, so her body was half out of the water, stretching, arching back, her pectoral fins outstretched, then falling backward with a massive splash that reached them on the boat and soaked them to the skin.

Neither of them noticed. Neither of them cared.

The whale was sinking now, deep, so deep that only a mass of still water on the surface showed her presence. Then she burst up one more time, arched back once more—and she dived once more and they saw her print on the water above as she adjusted course and headed for the horizon, her calf tearing after her.

Two wild creatures returned to the deep.

Tears were sliding uselessly down Jenny's face. She couldn't stop them, any more than she could stop smiling. And she looked up at Ramón and saw his smile echo hers.

'We did it,' she breathed. 'Ramón, we did it.'

'We did,' he said, and he tugged her hard against him, then swung her round so he was looking into her tear-stained face. 'We did it, Gianetta, we saved our whale. And you were magnificent. Gianetta, you may be a Spanish-Australian woman in name but I believe you have your nationality wrong. A woman like you... I believe you're worthy of being a woman of Cepheus.'

And then, before she knew what he intended, before she could guess anything at all, he lifted her into his arms and he kissed her.

CHAPTER FOUR

ONE moment she was gazing out at the horizon, catching the last shimmer of the whale's wake on the translucence of the sea. The next she was being kissed as she'd never been kissed in her life.

His hands were lifting her, pulling her hard in against him so her feet barely touched the deck. His body felt rock-hard, the muscled strength he'd just displayed still at work, only now directed straight at her. Straight with her.

The emotions of the rescue were all around her. He was wet and wild and wonderful. She was soaking as well, and the dripping fabric of his shirt and hers meant their bodies seemed to cling and melt.

It felt right. It felt meant. It felt as if there was no room or sense to argue.

His mouth met hers again, his arms tightening around her so she was locked hard against him. He was so close she could feel the rapid beat of his heart. Her breasts were crushed against his chest, her face had tilted instinctively, her mouth was caught…

Caught? Merged, more like. Two parts of a whole finding their home.

He tugged her tighter, tighter still against him, moulding her lips against his. She was hard against him, closer, closer, feeling him, tasting him, wanting him…

To be a part of him seemed suddenly as natural, as right,

as breathing. To be kissed by this man was an extension of what had just happened.

Or maybe it was more than that. Maybe it was an extension of the whole of the last week.

Maybe she'd wanted this from the moment she'd seen him.

Either way, she certainly wasn't objecting now. She heard herself give a tiny moan, almost a whimper, which was stupid because she didn't feel the least like whimpering. She felt like shouting, *Yes!*

His mouth was demanding, his tongue was searching for an entry, his arms holding her so tightly now he must surely bruise. But he couldn't hold her tight enough. She was holding him right back, desperate that she not be lowered, desperate that this miraculous contact not be lost.

He felt so good. He felt as if he was meant to be right here in her arms. That she'd been destined for this moment for ever and it had taken this long to find him.

He hadn't shaved this morning. She could feel the stubble on his jaw, she could almost taste it. There was salt on his face—of course there was, he'd been practically submerged, over and over. He smelled of salt and sea, and of pure testosterone.

He tasted of Ramón.

'Ramón.' She heard herself whisper his name, or maybe it was in her heart, for how could she possibly whisper when he was kissing as if he was a man starved for a woman, starved of *this* woman? She knew so clearly what was happening, and she accepted it with elation. This woman was who he wanted and he'd take her, he wanted her, she was his and he was claiming his own.

Like the whale rolling joyously in the sea, she thought, dazed and almost delirious, this was nature; it was right, it was meant.

She was in his arms and she wasn't letting go.

Ramón.

'Gianetta…' His voice was ragged with heat and desire.

Somehow he dragged himself back from her and held her at arm's length. 'Gianetta, *mia*…'

'If you're asking if I want you, then the answer's yes,' she said huskily, and almost laughed at the look of blazing heat that came straight back at her. His eyes were almost black, gleaming with tenderness and want and passion. But something else. He wouldn't take her yet. His eyes were searching.

'I'll take no woman against her will,' he growled.

'You think…you think this is against my will?' she whispered, as the blaze of desire became almost white-hot and she pressed herself against him, forcing him to see how much this was not the case.

'Gianetta,' he sighed, and there was laughter now as well as wonder and desire. Before she could respond he had her in his arms, held high, cradled against him, almost triumphant.

'You don't think maybe we should set the automatic pilot or something?' she murmured. 'We'll drift.'

'The radar will tell us if we're about to hit something big,' he said, his dark eyes gleaming. 'But it can't pick up things like jellyfish, so there's a risk. You want to risk death by jellyfish and come to my bed while we wait, my Gianetta?'

And what was a girl to say to an invitation like that?

'Yes, please,' she said simply and he kissed her and he held her tight and carried her down below.

To his bed. To his arms. To his pleasure.

'She left port six days ago, heading for New Zealand.'

The lawyer stared at the boat builder in consternation. 'You're sure? The *Marquita*?'

'That's the one. The guy skippering her—Ramón, I think he said his name was—had her in dry dock here for a couple of days, checking the hull, but she sailed out on the morning tide on Monday. Took the best cook in the bay with him, too. Half the locals are after his blood. He'd better look after our Jenny.'

But the lawyer wasn't interested in Ramón's staff. He stood

on the dock and stared out towards the harbour entrance as if he could see the *Marquita* sailing away.

'You're sure he was heading for Auckland?'

'I am. You're Spanish, right?'

'Cepheus country,' the lawyer said sharply. 'Not Spain. But no matter. How long would it take the *Marquita* to get to Auckland?'

'Coupla weeks,' the boat builder told him. 'Can't see him hurrying. I wouldn't hurry if I had a boat like the *Marquita* and Jenny aboard.'

'So if I go to Auckland…'

'I guess you'd meet him. If it's urgent.'

'It's urgent,' the lawyer said grimly. 'You have no idea how urgent.'

There was no urgency about the *Marquita*. If she took a year to reach Auckland it was too soon for Jenny.

Happiness was right now.

They could travel faster, but that would mean sitting by the wheel hour after hour, setting the sails to catch the slightest wind shift, being sailors.

Instead of being lovers.

She'd never felt like this. She'd melted against Ramón's body the morning of the whales and she felt as if she'd melted permanently. She'd shape shifted, from the Jenny she once knew to the Gianetta Ramón loved.

For that was what it felt like. Loved. For the first time in her life she felt truly beautiful, truly desirable—and it wasn't just for her body.

Yes, he made love to her, over and over, wonderful love-making that made her cry out in delight.

But more.

He wanted to know all about her.

He tugged blankets up on the deck. They lay in the sun and they solved the problems of the world. They watched dolphins surf in their wake. They fished. They compared toes to see whose little toe bent the most.

That might be ridiculous but there was serious stuff, too. Ramón now knew all about her parents, her life, her baby. She told him everything about Matty, she showed him pictures and he examined each of them with the air of a man being granted a privilege.

When Matty was smiling, Ramón smiled. She watched this big man respond to her baby's smile and she felt her heart twist in a way she'd never thought possible.

He let the boom net down off the rear deck, and they surfed behind the boat, and when the wind came up it felt as if they were flying. They worked the sails as a team, setting them so finely that they caught up on time lost when they were below, lost in each other's bodies.

He touched her and her body reacted with fire.

Don't fall in love. Don't fall in love. It was a mantra she said over and over in her head, but she knew it was hopeless. She was hopelessly lost.

It wouldn't last. Like Kieran, this man was a nomad, a sailor of no fixed address, going where the wind took him.

He talked little about himself. She knew there'd been tragedy, the sister he'd loved, parents he'd lost, pain to make him shy from emotional entanglement.

Well, maybe she'd learned that lesson, too. So savour the moment, she told herself. For now it was wonderful. Each morning she woke in Ramón's arms and she thought: Ramón had employed her for a year! When they got back to Europe conceivably the owner would join them. She could go back to being crew. But Ramón would be crew as well, and the nights were long, and owners never stayed aboard their boats for ever.

'Tell me about the guy who owns this boat,' she said, two days out of Auckland and she watched a shadow cross Ramón's face. She was starting to know him so well—she watched him when he didn't know it—his strongly boned, aquiline face, his hooded eyes, the smile lines, the weather lines from years at sea.

What had suddenly caused the shadow?

'He's rich,' he said shortly. 'He trusts me. What else do you need to know?'

'Well, whether he likes muffins, for a start,' she said, with something approaching asperity, which was a bit difficult as she happened to be entwined in Ramón's arms as she spoke and asperity was a bit hard to manage. Breathless was more like it.

'He loves muffins,' Ramón said.

'He'll be used to richer food than I can cook. Do you usually employ someone with special training?'

'He eats my cooking.'

'Really?' She frowned and sat up in bed, tugging the sheet after her. She'd seen enough of Ramón's culinary skills to know what an extraordinary statement this was. 'He's rich and he eats your cooking?'

'As I said, he'll love your muffins.'

'So when will you next see him?'

'Back in Europe,' Ramón said, and sighed. 'He'll have to surface then, but not now. Not yet. There's three months before we have to face the world. Do you think we can be happy for three months, *cariño*?' And he tugged her back down to him.

'If you keep calling me *cariño*,' she whispered. 'Are we really being paid for this?'

He chuckled but then his smile faded once more. 'You know it can't last, my love. I will need to move on.'

'Of course you will,' she whispered, but she only said it because it was the sensible, dignified thing to say. A girl had some pride.

Move on?

She never wanted to move on. If her world could stay on this boat, with this man, for ever, she wasn't arguing at all.

She slept and Ramón held her in his arms and tried to think of the future.

He didn't have to think. Not yet. It was three months before he was due to leave the boat and return to Bangladesh.

Three months before he needed to tell Jenny the truth.

She could stay with the boat, he thought, if she wanted to. He always employed someone to stay on board while he was away. She could take that role.

Only that meant Jenny would be in Cepheus while he was in Bangladesh.

He'd told her he needed to move on. It was the truth.

Maybe she could come with him.

The idea hit and stayed. His team always had volunteers to act as manual labour. Would Jenny enjoy the physical demands of construction, of helping make life bearable for those who had nothing?

Maybe she would.

What was he thinking? He'd never considered taking a woman to Bangladesh. He'd never considered that leaving a woman behind seemed unthinkable.

Gianetta...

His arms tightened their hold and she curved closer in sleep. He smiled and kissed the top of her head. Her curls were so soft.

Maybe he could sound her out about Bangladesh.

Give it time, he told himself, startled by the direction his thoughts were taking him. You've known her for less than two weeks.

Was it long enough?

There was plenty of time after Auckland. It was pretty much perfect right now, he thought. Let's not mess with perfection. He'd just hold this woman and hope that somehow the love he'd always told himself was an illusion might miraculously become real.

Anything was possible.

'How do you know he'll sail straight to Auckland?'

In the royal palace of Cepheus, Sofía was holding the telephone and staring into the middle distance, seeing not the magnificent suits of armour in the grand entrance but a vision of an elderly lawyer pacing anxiously on an unknown dock half a world away. She could understand his anxiety. Things in the palace were reaching crisis point.

The little boy had gone into foster care yesterday. Philippe needed love, Sofía thought bleakly. His neglect here—all his physical needs met, but no love, little affection, just a series of disinterested nannies—seemed tantamount to child abuse, and the country knew of it. She'd found him lovely foster parents, but his leaving the palace was sending the wrong message to the population—as if Ramón himself didn't care for the child.

Did Ramón even know about him?

'I don't know for sure where the Prince will sail,' the lawyer snapped. 'But I can hope. He'll want to restock fast to get around the Horn. It makes sense for him to come here.'

'So you'll wait.'

'Of course I'll wait. What else can I do?'

'But there's less than two weeks to go,' Sofía wailed. 'What if he's delayed?'

'Then we have catastrophe,' the lawyer said heavily. 'He has to get here. Then he has to get back to Cepheus and accept his new life.'

'And the child?'

'It doesn't matter about the child.'

Yes, it does, Sofía thought. Oh, Ramón, what are you facing?

They sailed into Auckland Harbour just after dawn. Jenny stood in the bow, ready to jump across to shore with the lines, ready to help in any way she could with berthing the *Marquita*. Ramón was at the wheel. She glanced back at him and had a pang of misgivings.

They hadn't been near land for two weeks. Why did it feel as if the world was waiting to crowd in?

How could it? Their plan was to restock and be gone again. Their idyll could continue.

But they'd booked a berth with the harbour master. Ramón

had spoken to the authorities an hour ago, and after that he'd looked worried.

'Problem?' she'd asked.

'Someone's looking for me.'

'Debt collectors?' she'd teased, but he hadn't smiled.

'I don't have debts.'

'Then who…?'

'I don't know,' he said, and his worry sounded as if it was increasing. 'No one knows where I am.'

'Conceivably the owner knows.'

'What…?' He caught himself. 'I…yes. But he won't be here. I can't think…'

That was all he'd said but she could see worry building.

She turned and looked towards the dock. She'd looked at the plan the harbour master had faxed through and from here she could see the berth that had been allocated to them.

There was someone standing on the dock, at the berth, as if waiting. A man in a suit.

It must be the owner, she thought.

She glanced back at Ramón and saw him flinch.

'Rodriguez,' he muttered, and in the calm of the early morning she heard him swear. 'Trouble.'

'Is he the boat's owner?'

'No,' he said shortly. 'He's legal counsel to the Crown of Cepheus. I've met him once or twice when he had business with my grandmother. If he's here… I hate to imagine what he wants of me.'

Señor Rodriguez was beside himself. He had ten days to save a country. He glanced at his watch as the *Marquita* sailed slowly towards her berth, fretting as if every second left was vital.

What useless display of skill was this, to sail into harbour when motoring would be faster? And why was the woman in the bow, rather than Ramón himself? He needed to talk to Ramón, now!

The boat edged nearer. 'Can you catch my line?' the

woman called, and he flinched and moved backward. He knew nothing about boats.

But it seemed she could manage without him. She jumped lightly over a gap he thought was far too wide, landing neatly on the dock, then hauled the boat into position and made her fast as Ramón tugged down the last sail.

'Good morning,' the woman said politely, casting him a curious glance. And maybe she was justified in her curiosity. He was in his customary suit, which he acknowledged looked out of place here. The woman was in the uniform of the sea—faded shorts, a T-shirt and nothing else. She looked wind-blown and free. Momentarily, he was caught by how good she looked, but only for an instant. His attention returned to Ramón.

'Señor Rodriguez,' Ramón called to him, cautious and wary.

'You remember me?'

'Yes,' Ramón said shortly. 'What's wrong?'

'Nothing's wrong,' the lawyer said, speaking in the mix of French and Spanish that formed the Cepheus language. 'As long as you come home.'

'My home's on the *Marquita*. You know that.'

'Not any more it's not,' the lawyer said. 'Your uncle and your cousin are dead. As of four weeks ago, you're the Crown Prince of Cepheus.'

There was silence. Jenny went on making all secure while Ramón stared at the man on the dock as if he'd spoken a foreign language.

Which he had, but Jenny had been raised speaking Spanish like a native, and she'd picked up French at school. There were so many similarities in form she'd slipped into it effortlessly. Now… She'd missed the odd word but she understood what the lawyer had said.

Or she thought she understood what he'd said.

Crown Prince of Cepheus. Ramón.

It might make linguistic sense. It didn't make any other sort of sense.

'My uncle's dead?' Ramón said at last, his voice without inflexion.

'In a light plane crash four weeks ago. Your uncle, your cousin and your cousin's wife, all killed. Only there's worse. It seems your cousin wasn't really married—he brought the woman he called his wife home and shocked his father and the country by declaring he was married, but now we've searched for proof, we've found none. So the child, Philippe, who stood to be heir, is illegitimate. You stand next in line. But if you're not home in ten days then Carlos inherits.'

'Carlos!' The look of flat shock left Ramón's face, replaced by anger, pure and savage. 'You're saying Carlos will inherit the throne?'

'Not if you come home. You must see that's the only way.'

'No!'

'Think about it.'

'I've thought.'

'Leave the woman to tend the boat and come with me,' Señor Rodriguez said urgently. 'We need to speak privately.'

'The woman's name is Gianetta.' Ramón's anger seemed to be building. 'I won't leave her.'

The man cast an uninterested glance at Jenny, as if she was of no import. Which, obviously, was the case. 'Regardless, you must come.'

'I can look after the boat,' Jenny said, trying really hard to keep up. *I won't leave her.* There was a declaration. But he obviously meant it for right now. Certainly not for tomorrow. *Crown Prince of Cepheus?*

'There's immigration…' Ramón said.

'I can sort my papers out,' she said. 'The harbour master's office is just over there. You do what you have to do on the way to wherever you're going. Have your discussion and then come back and tell me what's happening.'

'Jenny…'

But she was starting to add things together in her head and she wasn't liking them. *Crown Prince of Cepheus.*

'I guess the *Marquita* would be *your* boat, then?' she asked flatly, and she saw him flinch.

'Yes, but…'

She felt sick. 'There you go,' she managed, fighting for dignity. 'The owner's needs always come first. I'll stow the sails and make all neat. Then I might go for a nice long walk and let off a little steam. I'll see you later.'

And Ramón cast her a glance where frustration, anger—and maybe even a touch of envy—were combined.

'If you can…'

'Of course I can,' she said, almost cordially. 'We're on land again. I can stand on my own two feet.'

There were complications everywhere, and all he could think of was Jenny. Gianetta. His woman.

The flash of anger he'd seen when he'd confessed that he did indeed own the *Marquita*; the look of betrayal…

She'd think he'd lied to her. She wouldn't understand what else was going on, but the lie would be there, as if in flashing neon.

Yes, he'd lied.

He needed to concentrate on the lawyer.

The throne of Cepheus was his.

Up until now there'd never been a thought of him inheriting. Neither his uncle nor his cousin, Cristián, had ever invited Ramón near the palace. He knew the country had been in dread of Cristián becoming Crown Prince but there was nothing anyone could do about it. Cristián had solidified his inheritance by marrying and having a child. The boy must be what, five?

For him to be proved illegitimate…

'I can't even remember the child's name,' he said across the lawyer's stream of explanations, and the lawyer cast him a reproachful glance.

'Philippe.'

'How old?'

'Five,' he confirmed.

'So what happens to Philippe?'

'Nothing,' the lawyer said. 'He has no rights. With his parents dead, your aunt has organized foster care, and if you wish to make a financial settlement on him I imagine the country will be relieved. There's a certain amount of anger...'

'You mean my cousin didn't make provision for his own son?'

'Your cousin and your uncle spent every drop of their personal incomes on themselves, on gambling, on...on whatever they wished. The Crown itself, however, is very wealthy. You, with the fortune your grandmother left you and the Crown to take care of your every need, will be almost indecently rich. But the child has nothing.'

He felt sick. A five-year-old child. To lose everything...

He'd been not much older than Philippe when he'd lost his own father.

It couldn't matter. It shouldn't be his problem. He didn't even know the little boy...

'I'll take financial care of the child,' Ramón said shortly. 'But I can't drop everything. I have twelve more weeks at sea and then I'm due in Bangladesh.'

'Your team already knows you won't be accompanying them this year,' the lawyer told him flatly, leaving no room for argument. 'And I've found an experienced yachtsman who's prepared to sail the *Marquita* back to Cepheus for you. We can be on a flight tonight, and even that's not soon enough.' Then, as the lawyer noticed Ramón's face—and Ramón was making no effort to disguise his fury—he added quickly, 'There's mounting hysteria over the mess your uncle and cousin left, and there's massive disquiet about Carlos inheriting.'

'As well there might be,' Ramón growled, trying hard to stay calm. Ramón's distant cousin was an indolent gamester, rotund, corrupt and inept. He'd faced the court more than once, but charges had been dropped, because of bribery? He wasn't close enough to the throne to know.

'He's making noises that the throne should be his. Blustering threats against you and your aunt.'

'Threats?' And there it was again, the terror he'd been raised with. *'Don't go near the throne. Ever!'*

'If the people rise against the throne...' the lawyer was saying.

'Maybe that would be a good thing.'

'Maybe it'd be a disaster,' the man said, and proceeded to tell him why. At every word Ramón felt his world disintegrate. There was no getting around it—the country was in desperate need of a leader, of some sort of stability...of a Crown Prince.

'So you see,' the lawyer said at last, 'you have to come. Go back to the boat, tell the woman—she's your only crew?—what's happening, pack your bags and we'll head straight to the airport.'

And there was nothing left for him but to agree. To take his place in a palace that had cost his family everything.

'Tomorrow,' he said, feeling ill.

'Tonight.'

'I will spend tonight with Gianetta,' Ramón growled, and the lawyer raised his brows.

'Like that?'

'Like nothing,' Ramón snapped. 'She deserves an explanation.'

'It's not as if you're sacking her,' the lawyer said. 'I've only hired one man to replace you. She'll still be needed. She can help bring the *Marquita* home and then you can pay her off.'

'I've already paid her.'

'Then there's no problem.' The lawyer rose and so did Ramón. 'Tonight.'

'Tomorrow,' Ramón snapped and looked at the man's face and managed a grim smile. 'Consider it my first royal decree. Book the tickets for tomorrow's flights.'

'But...'

'I will not argue,' Ramón said. 'I've a mind to wash my hands of the whole business and take *Marquita* straight back out to sea.' Then, at the wash of undisguised distress on the lawyer's face, he sighed and relented. 'But, of course, I won't,' he said. 'You know I won't. I will return with you to Cepheus. I'll do what I must to resolve this mess, I'll face Carlos down, but you will give me one more night.'

CHAPTER FIVE

SHE walked for four long hours, and then she found an Internet café and did some research. By the time she returned to the boat she was tired and hungry and her anger hadn't abated one bit.

Ramón was the Crown Prince of Cepheus. What sort of dangerous mess had she walked into?

She'd slept with a prince?

Logically, it shouldn't make one whit of difference that he was royal, but it did, and she felt used and stupid and very much like a star-struck teenager. All that was needed was the paparazzi. Images of headlines flashed through her head—*Crown Prince of Cepheus Takes Stupid, Naive Australian Lover*—and as she neared the boat she couldn't help casting a furtive glance over her shoulder to check the thought had no foundation.

It didn't—of course it didn't. There was only Ramón, kneeling on the deck, calmly sealing the ends of new ropes.

He glanced up and saw her coming. He smiled a welcome, but she was too sick at heart to smile back.

For a few wonderful days she'd let herself believe this smile could be for her.

She felt besmirched.

'I've just come back to get my things,' she said flatly before he had a chance to speak.

'You're leaving?' His eyes were calmly appraising.

'Of course I'm leaving.'

'To go where?'

'I'll see if I can get a temporary job here. As soon as I can get back to Australia I'll organize some way of repaying the loan.'

'There's no need for you to repay...'

'There's every need,' she flashed, wanting to stamp her foot; wanting, quite badly, to cry. 'You think I want to be in your debt for one minute more than I must? I've read about you on the Internet now. It doesn't matter whether anyone died or not. You were a prince already.'

'Does that make a difference?' he asked, still watchful, and his very calmness added to her distress.

'Of course it does. I've been going to bed with a *prince*,' she wailed, and the couple on board their cruiser in the next berth choked on their lunch time Martinis.

But Ramón didn't notice. He had eyes only for her. 'You went to bed with me,' he said softly. 'Not with a prince.'

'You are a prince.'

'I'm just Ramón, Gianetta.'

'Don't Gianetta me,' she snapped. 'That's your bedroom we slept in. Not the owner's. Here I was thinking we were doing something illicit...'

'Weren't we?' he demanded and a glint of humour returned to his dark eyes.

'It was your bed all along,' she wailed and then, finally, she made a grab at composure. The couple on the next boat were likely to lose their eyes; they were out on stalks. Dignity, she told herself desperately. Please.

'So I own the boat,' he said. 'Yes, I'm a prince. What more do you know of me?'

'Apparently very little,' she said bitterly. 'I seem to have told you my whole life story. It appears you've only told me about two minutes of yours. Apparently you're wealthy, fabulously wealthy, and you're royal. The Internet bio was sketchy, but you spend your time either on this boat or fronting some charity organisation.'

'I do more than that.'

But she was past hearing. She was past wanting to hear. She felt humiliated to her socks, and one fact stood out above all the rest. *She'd never really known him.*

'So when you saw me you thought here's a little more charity,' she threw at him, anger making her almost incoherent. 'I'll take this poverty-stricken, flour-streaked muffin-maker and show her a nice time.'

'A flour-streaked muffin-maker?' he said and, infuriatingly, the laughter was back. 'I guess if you want to describe yourself as that… Okay, fine, I rescued the muffin-maker. And we did have a nice time. No?'

But she wasn't going there. She was not being sucked into that smile ever again. 'I'm leaving,' she said, and she swung herself down onto the deck. She was heading below, but Ramón was before her, blocking her path.

'Jenny, you're still contracted to take my boat to Cepheus.'

'You don't need me…'

'You signed a contract. Yesterday, as I remember—and it was you who wanted it signed before we came into port.' His hands were on her shoulders, forcing her to meet his gaze, and her anger was suddenly matched with his. 'So you've been on the Internet. Do you understand why I have to return?'

And she did understand. Sort of. She'd read and read and read. 'It seems your uncle and cousin are dead,' she said flatly. 'There's a huge scandal because it seems your cousin wasn't married after all, so his little son can't inherit. So you get to be Crown Prince.' Even now, she couldn't believe she was saying it. *Crown Prince.* It was like some appalling twisted fairy tale. Kiss a frog, have him turn into a prince.

She wanted her frog back.

'I don't have a choice in this,' he said harshly. 'You need to believe that.' Before she could stop him, he put the back of his hand against her cheek and ran it down to her lips, a touch so sensuous that it made a shiver run right down to her toes. But there was anger behind the touch—and there was also… Regret? 'Gianetta, for you to go…'

'Of course I'm going,' she managed.

'And I need to let you go,' he said, and there was a depth of sadness behind his words that she couldn't begin to understand. 'But still I want you to take my boat home. Selfish or not, I want to see you again.'

Where was dignity when she needed it? His touch had sucked all the anger out of her. She wanted to hold on to this man and cling.

What was she thinking? No. This man was royalty, and he'd lied to her.

She had to find sense.

'I'm grabbing my things,' she said shortly, fighting for some semblance of calm. 'I'll be in touch about the money. I swear I won't owe you for any longer than absolutely necessary.'

'There's no need to repay...'

'There is,' she snapped. 'I pay my debts, even if they're to princes.'

'Can you stop calling me...'

'A prince? It's what you are and it's not new. It's not like this title's a shock to you. Yes, you seem to have inherited the Crown, and that's surprised you, but you were born a prince and you didn't tell me.'

'You didn't ask.'

'Right,' she said, fury building again. She shoved his hands away and headed below, whether he liked it or not. Ramón followed her and stood watching as she flung her gear into her carry-all.

Dignity was nowhere. The only thing she could cling to was her anger.

'So, Jenny, you think I should have introduced myself as Prince Ramón?' he asked at last, and the anger was still there. He was angry? What did that make her? Nothing, she thought bleakly. How could he be angry at her? She felt like shrivelling into a small ball and sobbing, but she had to get away from here first.

'You know what matters most?' she demanded, trying desperately to sort her thoughts into some sort of sense. 'That you didn't tell me you owned the boat. Maybe you didn't lie outright, but you had plenty of opportunities to tell me and you didn't. That's a lie in my books.'

'Would you have got on my boat if you thought I was the owner?'

There was only one answer to that. If he'd asked her and she'd known he was wealthy enough to afford such a boat— his wealth would have terrified her. 'No,' she admitted.

'So I wanted you to come with me.'

'Bully for you. And I did.' Cling to the anger, she told herself. It was all there was. If he was angry, she should be more so. She headed into the bathroom to grab her toiletries. 'I came on board and we made love and it was all very nice,' she threw over her shoulder. 'Now you've had your fun and you can go back to your life.'

'Being a prince isn't my life.'

'No?'

'Gianetta…'

'Jenny!'

'Jenny, then,' he conceded and the underlying anger in his voice intensified. 'I want you to listen.'

'I'm listening,' she said, shoving toiletries together with venom.

'Jenny, my grandfather was the Crown Prince of Cepheus.'

'I know that.'

'What you don't know,' he snapped, 'is that he was an arrogant, cruel womanizer. Jenny, I need you to understand this. My grandfather's marriage to my grandmother was an arranged one and he treated her dreadfully. When my father was ten my grandmother fell in love with a servant, and who can blame her? But my grandfather banished her and the younger children to a tiny island off the coast of Cepheus. He kept his oldest son, my uncle, at the palace, but my grandmother, my father and my aunt were never allowed back. My grandmother was royal in her own right. She had money of her own and all her life she ached to undo some of the appalling things my grandfather did, but when she tried…well, that's when my father died. And now, to be forced to go back…'

'I'm sorry you don't like it,' she said stiffly. What was he explaining this for? It had nothing to do with her. 'But your country needs you. At least now you'll be doing something useful.'

'Is that what you think?' he demanded, sounding stunned. 'That I spend my life doing nothing?'

'Isn't that the best job in the world?' She could feel the vibrations of his anger and it fed hers. *He'd known he was a prince.* 'The Internet bio says you're aligned to some sort of charity in Bangladesh,' she said shortly. 'I guess you can't be all bad.'

'Thanks.'

'Think nothing of it,' she said, and she thought, where did she go from here?

Away, her head told her, harshly and coldly. She needed to leave right now, and she would, but there were obligations. This man had got her out of a hole. He'd paid her debts. She owed him, deception or not.

'Okay, I'll be the first to admit I know nothing of your life,' she said stiffly. 'I felt like I knew you and now I realize I don't. That hurts. But I do need to thank you for paying my debt; for getting me away from Charlie. But now I'm just…scared. So I'll just get out of your life and let you get on with it.'

'You're scared?'

'What do you think?'

'There's no threat. There'd only be a threat if you were my woman.'

That was enough to take her breath away. *If you were my woman…*

'Which…which I'm not,' she managed.

'No,' he said, and there was bleakness as well as anger there now.

She closed her eyes. So what else had she expected? These two weeks had been a fairy tale. Nothing more.

Move on.

'Jenny, I have to do this,' he said harshly. 'Understand it or not, this is what I'm faced with. If I don't take the throne, then it goes to my father's cousin's son, Carlos. Carlos is as bad as my grandfather. He'd bring the country to ruin. And then there's the child. He's five. God knows...' He raked his hair with quiet despair. 'I will accept this responsibility. I must, even if it means walking away from what I most care about.'

And then there was silence, stretching towards infinity, where only emptiness beckoned.

What he most cared about? His boat? His charity work? What?

She couldn't think of what. She couldn't think what she wanted *what* to be.

'I'm sorry, Ramón,' she whispered at last.

'I'm sorry, too,' he said. He sighed and dug his hands deep into his pockets. Seemingly moving on. 'For what's between us needs to be put aside, for the sanity of both of us. But Gianetta...Jenny... What will you do in New Zealand?'

'Make muffins.' Her fury from his perceived betrayal was oozing away now, but there was nothing in its place except an aching void. Yesterday had seemed so wonderful. Today her sailor had turned into a prince and her bubble of euphoria was gone.

'Make muffins until you can afford to go back to Australia?'

'I don't have a lot of choice.'

'There is. Señor Rodriguez, the lawyer you met this morning, has already found someone prepared to skipper the *Marquita*—to bring her to Cepheus. I've already met him. He's a Scottish Australian, Gordon, ex-merchant navy. He's competent, solid and I know I can trust him with...with my boat. But he will need crew. So I'm asking you to stay on. I'm asking you if you'll sail round the Horn with him and bring the *Marquita* home. If you do that, I'll fly you back to Australia. Debt discharged.'

'It wouldn't be discharged.'

'I believe it would,' he said heavily. 'I'm asking you to sail round the Horn with someone you don't know, and I'm asking you to trust that I'll keep my word. That's enough of a request to make paying out your debt more than reasonable.'

'I don't want to.'

'Do you want to go back to cooking muffins?' He spread his hands and he managed a smile then, his wonderful, sexy, insinuating smile that had the power to warm every last part of her. 'And at least this way you'll get to see Cepheus, even if it's only for a couple of days before you fly home. And you'll have sailed around the Horn. You wanted to see the world. Give yourself a chance to see a little of it.' He hesitated. 'And, Jenny, maybe…we can have tonight?'

That made her gasp. After all that stood between them… What was he suggesting, that she spend one more night as the royal mistress? 'Are you crazy?'

'So not tonight?' His eyes grew bleak. 'No. I'm sorry, Gianetta. You and me… I concede it's impossible. But what is possible is that you remain on board the *Marquita* as crew. You allow me to continue employing you so you'll walk away at the end of three months beholden to nobody.'

No.

The word should have been shouted at him. She should walk away right now.

But to walk away for ever? How could she do that? And if she stayed on board….maybe a sliver of hope remained.

Hope for what? A Cinderella happy ending? What a joke. Ramón himself had said it was impossible.

But to walk away, from this boat as well as from this man… Cinders had fled at midnight. Maybe Cinders had more resolution than she did.

'I'll come back to the boat in the morning,' she whispered. 'If the new skipper wants to employ me and I think he's a man I can be at sea with for three months…'

'He's nothing like me,' Ramón said gently, almost bleakly. 'He's reliable and steady.'

'And not a prince?'

He gave a wintry smile. 'No, Gianetta, he's not a prince.'

'Then it might be possible.'

'I hope it will be possible.'

'No guarantees,' she said.

'You feel betrayed?'

'Of course I do,' she whispered. 'I need to go now.'

The bleakness intensified. He nodded. 'As you say. Go, my Gianetta, before I forget myself. I've learned this day that my life's not my own. But first… '

And, before she could guess what he was about, he made two swift strides across the room, took her shoulders in a grip of iron and kissed her. And such a kiss… It was fierce, it was possessive, it held anger and passion and desire. It was no kiss of farewell. It was a kiss that was all about his need, his desire, his ache to hold her to him for this night, and for longer still.

He was hungry for her, she thought, bewildered. She didn't know how real that hunger was, but when he finally put her away from him, when she finally broke free, she thought he was hurting as much as she was.

But hunger changed nothing, she thought bleakly. There was nothing left to say.

He stood silently by as she grabbed her carry-all and walked away, her eyes shimmering with unshed tears. He didn't try to stop her.

He was her Ramón, she thought bleakly. But he wasn't her prince.

He watched her go, walking along the docks carrying her holdall, her shoulders slumped, her body language that of someone weary beyond belief.

He felt as if he'd betrayed her.

So what to do? Go after her, lift her bodily into his arms? Take her to Cepheus?

How could he?

There were threats from Carlos. The lawyer was talking of

the possibility of armed insurrection against the throne. Had it truly become so bad?

His father had died because he hadn't realized the power of royalty. How could he drag a woman into this mess? It would be hard enough keeping himself afloat, let alone supporting anyone else.

How could he be a part of it himself—a royal family that had destroyed his family?

Jenny's figure was growing smaller in the distance. She wasn't pausing—she wasn't looking back.

He felt ill.

'So can we leave tonight?' He looked back and the lawyer was standing about twenty feet from the boat, calmly watching. 'I asked them to hold seats on tonight's flight as well as tomorrow.'

'You have some nerve.'

'The country's desperate,' the lawyer said simply. 'Nothing's been heard from you. Carlos is starting to act as if he's the new Crown Prince and his actions are provocative. Delay on your part may well mean bloodshed.'

'I don't want to leave her,' he said simply and turned back—but she'd turned a corner and was gone.

'I think the lady has left you,' the lawyer said gently. 'Which leaves you free to begin to govern your country. So, the flight tonight, Your Highness?'

'Fine,' Ramón said heavily and went to pack.

But fine was the last thing he was feeling.

His flight left that evening. He looked down from the plane and saw the boats in Auckland Harbour. The *Marquita* was down there with her new skipper on board. He couldn't make her out among so many. She was already dwindling to nothing as the plane rose and turned away from land.

Would Jenny join her tomorrow, he thought bleakly. Would she come to Cepheus?

He turned from the window with a silent oath. It shouldn't

matter. What was between them was finished. Whether she broke her contract or not—there was nothing he could offer her.

Jenny was on her own, as was he.

His throne was waiting for him.

And two days later the *Marquita* slipped its moorings and sailed out of Auckland Harbour—with Jenny still on board. As she watched the harbour fade into the distance she felt all the doubts reassemble themselves. Gordon, her new skipper, seemed respectful of her silence and he let her be.

She was about to sail around the Horn. Once upon a time that prospect would have filled her with adrenalin-loaded excitement.

Now… She was simply fulfilling a contract, before she went home.

CHAPTER SIX

RAMÓN'S introduction to royal life was overwhelming. He walked into chaos. He walked into a life he knew nothing about. There were problems everywhere, but he'd been back in Cepheus for less than a day before the plight of Philippe caught him and held.

On his first meeting, the lawyer's introduction to the little boy was brief. 'This is Philippe.'

Philippe. His cousin's son. The little boy who should be Crown Prince, but for the trifling matter of a lack of wedding vows. Philippe, who'd had the royal surname until a month ago and was now not entitled to use it.

The little boy looked like the child Ramón remembered being. Philippe's pale face and huge eyes hinted that he was suffering as Ramón had suffered when his own father died, and as he met him for the first time he felt his gut wrench with remembered pain.

He'd come to see for himself what he'd been told—that the little boy was in the best care possible. Señor Rodriguez performed the introductions. Consuela and Ernesto were Philippe's foster parents, farmers who lived fifteen minutes' drive from the palace. The three were clearly nervous of what this meeting meant, but Philippe had been well trained.

'I am pleased to meet you,' the little boy said in a stilted little voice that spoke of rote learning and little else. He held out a thin little arm so his hand could be shaken, and Ramón felt him flinch as he took it in his.

Philippe's foster mother, a buxom farmer's wife exuding good-hearted friendliness, didn't seem intimidated by Ramón's title, or maybe she was, but her concern for Philippe came first. 'We've been hearing good things about you,' she told Ramón, scooping her charge into her arms so he could be on eye level with Ramón, ending the formality with this decisive gesture. 'This dumpling's been fearful of meeting you,' she told him. 'But Ernesto and I are telling him he should think of you as his big cousin. A friend. Isn't that right, Your Highness?'

She met Ramón's gaze almost defiantly, and Ramón could see immediately why Sofía had chosen Consuela as Philippe's foster mother. The image of a mother hen, prepared to battle any odds for her chick, was unmistakable. 'Philippe's homesick for the palace,' she said now, almost aggressively. 'And he misses his cat.'

'You have a cat?' Ramón asked.

'Yes,' Philippe whispered.

'There are many cats at the palace,' Señor Rodriguez said repressively from beside them, and Ramón sighed. What was it with adults? Hang on, he was an adult. Surely he could do something about this.

He must.

But he wasn't taking him back to the palace.

Memories were flooding back as he watched Philippe, memories of himself as a child. He vaguely remembered someone explaining that his grandmother wanted to return to the palace and his father would organize it—or maybe that explanation had come later. What he did remember was his father leading him into the vast grand entrance of the palace, Ramón clutching his father's hand as the splendour threatened to overwhelm him. 'There's nothing to be afraid of. It's time you met your grandfather and your uncle,' his father had told him.

His mother had said later that the decision to take him had been made, 'Because surely the Prince can't refuse his grandchild, a little boy who looks just like him.' But his mother had been wrong.

Not only had he been refused, some time in the night while Ramón lay in scared solitude, in a room far too grand for a child, somehow, some time, his father had died. He remembered not sleeping all night, and the next morning he remembered his grandfather, his icy voice laced with indifference to both his son's death and his grandson's solitary grief, snarling at the servants. 'Pack him up and get him out of here,' he'd ordered.

Pack him up and get him out of here... It was a dreadful decree, but how much worse would it have been if the Crown Prince had ordered him to stay? As he was being ordered to stay now.

Not Philippe, though. Philippe was free, if he could just be made happy with that freedom.

'Tell me about your cat,' he asked, trying a smile, and Philippe swallowed and swallowed again and made a manful effort to respond.

'He's little,' he whispered. 'The other cats fight him and he's not very strong. Something bit his ear. Papà doesn't permit me to take him inside, so he lives in the stables, but he comes when I call him. He's orange with a white nose.'

'Are there many orange cats with white noses at the palace?' Ramón asked, and for some reason the image of Jenny was with him strongly, urging him on. The little boy shook his head.

'Bebe's the only one. He's my friend.' He tilted his chin, obviously searching for courage for a confession. 'Sometimes I take a little fish from the kitchen when no one's looking. Bebe likes fish.'

'So he shouldn't be hard to find.' Ramón glanced at Consuela and Ernesto, questioningly. This place was a farm. Surely one cat...

'We like cats,' Consuela said, guessing where he was going. 'But Señor Rodriguez tells us the palace cats are wild.

They're used to keep the vermin down and he says no one can catch one, much less tame one.'

'I'm sure we could tame him.' Ernesto, a wiry, weathered farmer, spoke almost as defiantly as his wife. 'If you, sir, or your staff, could try to catch him for us…'

'I'll try,' Ramón said. 'He's called Bebe, you say? My aunt has her cat at the palace now. She understands them. Let's see what we can do.'

Jenny would approve, he thought, as he returned to the palace, but he pushed the idea away. This was *his* challenge, as was every challenge in this place. It was nothing to do with Jenny.

As soon as he returned to the palace he raided the kitchens. Then he set off to the stables with a platter of smoked salmon. He set down the saucer and waited for a little ginger cat with a torn ear to appear. It took a whole three minutes.

Bebe wasn't wild at all. He stroked his ears and Bebe purred. He then shed ginger fur everywhere while he wrapped himself around Ramón's legs and the chair legs in the palace entrance and the legs of the footman on duty. Jenny would laugh, Ramón thought, but he shoved that thought away as well. Just do what comes next. *Do not think of Jenny.*

Bebe objected—loudly—to the ride in a crate on the passenger seat of Ramón's Boxster, but he settled into life with Philippe—'as if Philippe's been sneaking him into his bed for the last couple of years,' Consuela told him, and maybe he had.

After that, Philippe regained a little colour, but he still looked haunted. He missed the palace, he confided, as Ramón tried to draw him out. In a world of adults who hadn't cared, the palace itself had become his stability.

Pack him up and get him out of here…

It made sense, Ramón thought. If the servants' reaction to Philippe was anything to go by, he'd be treated like illegitimate dirt in the palace. And then there was his main worry, or maybe it wasn't so much a worry but a cold, hard certainty.

There was so much to be done in this country that his role

as Crown Prince overwhelmed him. He had to take it on; he had no choice, but in order to do it he must be clear-headed, disciplined, focused.

There was no link between love and duty in this job. He'd seen that spelled out with bleak cruelty. His grandmother had entered the palace through love, and had left it with her dreams and her family destroyed. His father had tried again to enter the palace, for the love of his mother, and he'd lost his life because of it. There were threats around him now, veiled threats, and who knew what else besides?

And the knowledge settled on his heart like grey fog. To stay focused on what he must do, he could put no other person at risk. Sofia was staying until after the coronation. After that she'd leave and no one would be at risk but him. He'd have no distractions and without them maybe, just maybe, he could bring this country back to the prosperity it deserved.

But Philippe… And Jenny?

They'd get over it, he told himself roughly. Or Philippe would get over his grief and move on. Jenny must never be allowed to know that grief.

And once again he told himself harshly, this was nothing to do with Jenny. There'd never been a suggestion that they take things further. Nor could there be. This was his life and his life only, even if it was stifling.

This place was stifling. Nothing seemed to have changed since his grandfather's reign, or maybe since long before.

Lack of change didn't mean the palace had been allowed to fall into disrepair, though. Even though his grandfather and uncle had overspent their personal fortunes, the Crown itself was still wealthy, so pomp and splendour had been maintained. Furnishings were still opulent, rich paintings still covered the walls, the woodwork gleamed and the paintwork shone. The staff looked magnificent, even if their uniforms had been designed in the nineteenth century.

But the magnificence couldn't disguise the fact that every one of the people working in this palace went about their duties with impassive faces. Any attempt by Ramón to penetrate their rigid facades was met with stony silence and, as the weeks turned into a month and then two, he couldn't make inroads into that rigidity.

The servants—and the country—seemed to accept him with passive indifference. He might be better than what had gone before, the newspapers declared, but he was still royal. Soon, the press implied, he'd become just like the others.

When he officially took his place as Crown Prince, he could make things better for the people of this county. He knew that, so he'd bear the opulence of the palace, the lack of freedom. He'd bear the formality and the media attention. He'd cope also with the blustering threats of a still furious Carlos; along with the insidious sense that threats like this had killed his father. He'd face them down.

Alone.

Once Philippe had recovered from his first grief, surely he'd be happy on the farm with Consuela and Ernesto.

And also... Jenny would be happy as a muffin-maker?

Why did he even think of her? Why had he ever insisted that she come here? It would have been easier for both of them if he'd simply let her go.

For she was Jenny, he reminded himself harshly, a dozen times a day. She was not Gianetta. She was free to go wherever she willed. She was Jenny, with the world at her feet.

Yet he watched the *Marquita*'s progress with an anxiety that bordered on obsession, and he knew that when Jenny arrived he would see her one last time. He must.

Was that wise?

He knew it wasn't. There was no place for Jenny here, as there was no place for Philippe.

He'd been alone for much of his adult life. He could go on being alone.

But he'd see Jenny once again first. Sensible or not.

Please...

Eleven weeks and two days after setting sail from Auckland, the *Marquita* sailed into Cepheus harbour and found a party.

As they approached land, every boat they passed, from tiny pleasure craft to workmanlike fishing vessels, was adorned in red, gold and deep, deep blue. The flag of Cepheus hung from every mast. The harbour was ringed with flags. There were people crowded onto the docks, spilling out of harbourside restaurants. Every restaurant looked crammed to bursting. It looked like Sydney Harbour on a sunny Sunday, multiplied by about a hundred, Jenny thought, dazed, as she made the lines ready to dock.

'You reckon they're here to welcome us?' Gordon called to her, and she smiled.

She'd become very fond of Gordon. When she'd first met him, the morning after Ramón had left, she'd been ready to walk away. Only his shy smile, his assumption that she was coming with him and his pleasure that she was, had kept her on board. He reminded her of her father. Which helped.

She'd been sailing with him now for almost three months. He'd kept his own counsel and she'd kept hers, and it had taken almost all those months for her emotions to settle.

Now…approaching the dock she was so tense she could hardly speak. Normally she welcomed Gordon's reserve but his silence was only adding to her tension.

There was no need for her to be tense, she told herself. She'd had a couple of surreal weeks with royalty. In true princely fashion he'd rescued her from a life of making muffins, and now she could get on with her life.

With this experience of sailing round the Horn behind her, and with Gordon's references, maybe she could get another job on board a boat. She could keep right on sailing. While Ramón…

See, that was what she couldn't let herself think. The future and Ramón.

It had been a two-week affair. Nothing more.

'What's the occasion?' Gordon was behind the wheel, calling to people on the boat passing them. But they didn't understand English, or Gordon's broad mixed accent.

'Why the flags and decorations?' she called in Spanish and was rewarded by comprehension.

'Are you from another planet?' they called, incredulous. 'Everyone knows what's happening today.'

Their language was the mix of Spanish and French Ramón had used with the lawyer. She felt almost at home.

No. This was Ramón's home. Not hers.

'We're from Australia,' she called. 'We know nothing.'

'Well, welcome.' The people raised glasses in salutation. 'You're here just in time.'

'For what?'

'For the coronation,' they called. 'It's a public holiday. Crown Prince Ramón Cavellero of Cepheus accepts his Crown today.'

Right. She stood in the bow and let her hands automatically organize lines. Or not. She didn't know what her hands were doing.

First thought? Stupidly, it was that Ramón wouldn't be meeting her.

Had she ever believed he would? Ramón was a Prince of the Blood. He'd have moved on.

'Is that our berth?' Gordon called, and she caught herself, glanced at the sheet the harbour master had faxed through and then looked ahead to where their designated berth should be.

And drew in her breath.

Ramón wasn't there. Of course he wasn't. But there was a welcoming committee. There were four officials, three men and a woman, all in some sort of official uniform. The colours of their uniform matched the colours of the flags.

This yacht belonged to royalty, and representatives of royalty were there to meet them.

'Reckon any of them can catch a line?' Gordon called and she tried to smile.

'We're about to find out.'

Not only could they catch a line, they were efficient, courteous and they took smoothly over from the time the *Marquita* touched the dock.

'Welcome,' the senior official said gravely, in English. 'You are exactly on time.'

'You've been waiting for us?'

'His Highness has had you tracked from the moment you left Auckland. He's delighted you could be here today. He asks that you attend the ceremony this afternoon, and the official ball this evening.'

Jenny swung around to stare at Gordon—who was staring back at her. They matched. They both had their mouths wide open.

'Reckon we won't fit in,' Gordon drawled at last, sounding flabbergasted. 'Reckon there won't be a lot of folk wearing salt-crusted oilskins on your guest list.'

'That's why we're here,' the official said smoothly. 'Jorge here will complete the care of the *Marquita*, while Dalila and Rudi are instructed to care for you. If you agree, we'll escort you to the palace, you'll be fitted with clothing suitable for the occasion and you'll be His Highness's honoured guests at the ceremonies this afternoon and this evening.'

Jenny gasped. Her head was starting to explode. To see Ramón as a prince...

'We can't,' Gordon muttered.

But Jenny looked at the elderly seaman and saw her mixture of emotions reflected on his face. They'd been at sea for three months now, and she knew enough of Gordon to realize he stacked up life's events and used them to fill the long stretches at sea that he lived for.

He was staring at the officials with a mixture of awe and dread. And desire.

If she didn't go, Gordon wouldn't go.

And, a little voice inside her breathed, she'd get to see Ramón one last time.

Once upon a time Ramón had been her skipper. Once upon a time he'd been her lover. He'd moved on now. He was a Crown Prince.

She'd see him today and then she'd leave.

* * *

For the *Marquita* to berth on the same day as his coronation was a coincidence he couldn't ignore, making his resolution waver.

He'd made the decision to send his apologies when the boat berthed, for Jenny to be treated with all honour, paid handsomely and then escorted to the airport and given a first-class ticket back to Australia. That was the sensible decision. He couldn't allow himself to be diverted from his chosen path. But when he'd learned the *Marquita*'s date of arrival was today he'd given orders before he thought it through. Sensible or not, he would see Jenny this one last time.

Maybe he should see it as an omen, he decided as he dressed. Maybe he was meant to have her nearby, giving him strength to take this final step.

Servants were fussing over his uniform, making sure he looked every inch the Ruler of Cepheus, and outside there was sufficient security to defend him against a small army. Carlos's blustering threats of support from the military seemed to have no foundation. On his own he had nothing to fear, and on his own he must rule.

The last three months had cemented his determination to change this country. If he must accept the Crown then he'd do it as it was meant to be done. He could change this country for the better. He could make life easier for the population. The Crown, this ultimate position of authority, had been abused for generations. If anyone was to change it, it must be him.

Duty and desire had no place together. He knew that, and the last months' assessment of the state of the country told him that his duty was here. He had to stay focused. *He didn't need Jenny.*

But, need her or not, he wanted Jenny at the ceremony. To have her come all this way and not see her—on this of all days—*that* was more unthinkable than anything.

He would dance with her this night, he thought. Just this once, he'd touch her and then he'd move forward. Alone.

The doors were swinging open. The Master of State was waiting. Cepheus was waiting.

He'd set steps in place to bring this country into the twenty-first century, he thought with grim satisfaction. His coronation would cement those steps. Fulfilling the plans he'd set in place over the last few weeks would mean this country would thrive.

But maybe the population would never forget the family he came from, he thought as he was led in stately grandeur to the royal carriage. There were no cheers, no personal applause. Today the country was celebrating a public holiday and a continuum of history, but the populace wasn't impressed by what he personally represented. His grandfather's reputation came before him, smirching everything. Royalty was something to be endured.

The country had celebrated the birth of a new Crown Prince five years ago. That deception still rankled, souring all.

Philippe should be here, he thought. The little boy should play some part in this ceremony.

But, out at the farm, Philippe was finally starting to relax with him, learning again to be a little boy. He still missed the palace, but to bring him back seemed just as impossible as it had been three months ago.

Philippe was now an outsider. As he was himself, he thought grimly, glancing down at his uniform that made him seem almost ludicrously regal. And the threats were there, real or not.

He could protect Philippe. He *would* protect Philippe, but from a distance. Jenny was here for this day only. Sofía would be gone. He could rule as he needed to rule.

'It's time, Your Highness,' the Head of State said in stentorian tones, and Ramón knew that it was.

It was time to accept that he was a Prince of the Blood, with all the responsibility—and loss—that the title implied.

The great chorus of trumpets sounded, heralding the beginning of ceremonies and Jenny was sitting in a pew in the vast cathedral of Cepheus feeling bewildered. Feeling transformed. Feeling like Cinderella must have felt after the fairy godmother waved her wand.

For she wasn't at the back with the hired help. She and Gordon were being treated like royalty themselves.

The palace itself had been enough to take her breath away, all spirals and turrets and battlements, a medieval fantasy clinging to white stone cliffs above a sea so blue it seemed to almost merge with the sky.

The apartment she'd been taken to within the palace had taken even more of her breath away. It was as big as a small house, and Gordon had been shown into a similar one on the other side of the corridor. Corridor? It was more like a great hall. You could play a football match in the vast areas—decorated in gold, all carvings, columns and ancestral paintings—that joined the rooms. Dalila had ushered her in, put her holdall on a side table and instructed a maid to unpack.

'I'm not staying here,' Jenny had gasped.

'For tonight at least,' Dalila had said, formally polite in stilted English. 'The ball will be late. The Prince requires you to stay.'

How to fight a decree like that? How indeed to fight, when clothes were being produced that made her gasp all over again.

'I can't wear these.'

'You can,' the woman decreed. 'If you'll just stay still. Dolores is a dressmaker. It will take her only moments to adjust these for size.'

And Jenny had simply been too overwhelmed to refuse. So here she was, in a pew ten seats from the front, right on the aisle, dressed in a crimson silk ball-gown that looked as if it had been made for her. It was cut low across her breasts, with tiny capped sleeves, the bodice clinging like a second skin, curving to her hips and then flaring out to an almost full circle skirt. The fabric was so beautiful it made her feel as if she was floating.

There was a pendant round her neck that she hoped was paste but she suspected was a diamond so big she couldn't comprehend it. Her hair was pinned up in a deceptively simple knot and her make-up had been applied with a skill so great that when she looked in the mirror she saw someone she didn't recognize.

She felt like…Gianetta. For the first time in her life, her father's name seemed right for her.

'I'm just glad they can't see me back at the Sailor's Arms in Auckland,' Gordon muttered, and she glanced at the weathered seaman who looked as classy as she did, in a deep black suit that fitted him like a glove. He, too, had been transformed, like it or not. She almost chuckled, but then the music rose to a crescendo and she stopped thinking about chuckling. She stopped thinking about anything at all—anything but Ramón.

Crown Prince Ramón Cavellero of Cepheus.

For so he was.

The great doors of the cathedral had swung open. The Archbishop of Cepheus led the way in stately procession down the aisle, and Ramón trod behind, intent, his face set in lines that said this was an occasion of such great moment that lives would change because of it.

He truly was a prince, she thought, dazed beyond belief. If she'd walked past him in the street—no, if she'd seen his picture on the cover of a magazine, for this wasn't a man one passed in the street, she would never have recognized him. His uniform was black as night, skilfully cut to mould to his tall, lean frame. The leggings, the boots, the slashes of gold, the tassels, the fierce sword at his side, they only accentuated his aura of power and strength and purpose.

Or then again…maybe she would have recognized him. His eyes seemed to have lost their colour—they were dark as night. His mouth was set and grim, and it was the expression she'd seen when he'd known she was leaving.

He looked like…an eagle, she thought, a fierce bird of prey, ready to take on the world. But he was still Ramón.

He was so near her now. If she put out her hand…

He was passing her row. He was right here. And as he passed… His gaze shifted just a little from looking steadily ahead. Somehow it met hers and held, for a nano-second, for a fraction that might well be imagined. And then he was gone, swept past in the procession and the world crowded back in.

He hadn't smiled, but had his grimness lifted, just a little?

'He was looking for you,' Gordon muttered, awed. 'The guy who helped me dress said he told the aides where we were to sit. It's like we're important. Are you important to him then, lass?'

'Not in a million years,' she breathed.

She'd come.

It was the only thing holding him steady.

Gianetta. Jenny.

Her name was in his mind, like a mantra, said over and over.

'By the power vested in me…'

He was kneeling before the archbishop and the crown was being placed on his head. The weight was enormous.

She was here.

He could take this nowhere. He knew that. But still, for now, she was here on this day when he needed her most.

She was here, and his crown was the lighter for it.

The night seemed to be organized for her. As the throng emerged from the great cathedral, an aide appeared and took her arm.

'You're to come this way, miss. And you, too, sir,' he said to Gordon. 'You're official guests at the Coronation Dinner.'

'I reckon I'll slope back down to the boat,' Gordon muttered, shrinking, but Jenny clutched him as if she were drowning.

'We went round the Horn together,' she muttered. 'We face risk together.'

'This is worse than the Horn.'

'You're telling me,' Jenny said, and the aide was ushering them forward and it was too late to escape.

They sat, midway down a vast banquet table, where it

seemed half the world's dignitaries were assembled. Gordon, a seaman capable of facing down the world's worst storms, was practically shrinking under the table. Jenny was a bit braver, but not much. She was recognizing faces and names and her eyes grew rounder and rounder as she realized just who was here. There were speeches—of course—and she translated for Gordon and was glad of the task. It took her mind off what was happening.

It never took her mind off Ramón.

He was seated at the great formal table at the head of the room, gravely surveying all. He looked born to the role, she thought. He listened with gravitas and with courtesy. He paid attention to the two women on either side of him—grand dames, both of them, queens of their own countries.

'I have friends back in Australia who are never going to believe what I've done tonight,' she whispered to Gordon and her skipper nodded agreement.

Then once more the aide was beside them, bending to whisper to Jenny.

'Ma'am, I've been instructed to ask if you can waltz.'

'If I can…?'

'His Royal Highness wishes to dance with you. He doesn't wish to embarrass you, however, so if there's a problem…'

No. She wanted to scream, *no.*

But she glanced up at the head table and Ramón was watching her. Those eagle eyes were steady. 'I dare you,' his gaze was saying, and more.

'I can waltz,' she heard herself say, her eyes not leaving Ramón's.

'Excellent,' the aide said. 'I'll come to fetch you when we're ready.'

'You do that,' she said faintly.

What have I done?

The entrance to the grand ballroom was made in state. Ramón led the procession, and it was done in order of rank, which meant Jenny came in somewhere near the rear. Even that was intimidating—all the guests who hadn't been at the dinner were assembled in line to usher the dining party in.

If the ground opened up and swallowed her she'd be truly grateful. Too many people were looking at her.

Why had she agreed to dance?

Ramón was so far ahead she couldn't see him. Ramón. Prince Ramón.

She wasn't into fairy tales. Bring on midnight.

And Gordon had deserted her. As she took the aide's arm, as she joined the procession, he suddenly wasn't there. She looked wildly around and he was smiling apologetically but backing firmly away. But she was being ushered forward and there was no way she could run without causing a spectacle.

Cinderella ran, she thought wildly. At midnight.

But midnight was still a long time away.

Courage. If Cinders could face them all down, so could she. She took a deep breath and allowed herself to be led forward. The aide was ushering her into the ballroom, then into an alcove near the entrance. Before them, Ramón was making a grand sweep of the room, greeting everyone. The heads of the royal houses of Europe were his entourage, nodding, smiling, doing what royalty did best.

And suddenly she realized what was happening. Why she'd been directed to stand here. She was close to the door, where Ramón must end his circuit.

She felt frozen to the spot.

Ramón. Prince Ramón.

Ramón.

The wait was interminable. She tried to focus on anything but what was happening. A spot on the wax of the polished floor. The hem of her gown. Anything.

But finally, inevitably, the aide was beside her, ushering her forward and Ramón was right in front of her. Every eye in the room was on him. Every eye in the room was on her.

She was Jenny. She made muffins. She wanted to have hysterics, or faint.

Ramón was before her, his eyes grave and questioning.

'Gianetta,' he said softly, and every ear in the room was straining to hear. 'You've arrived for my coronation, and I thank you. You've brought my boat home and thus you've linked my old life with my new. Can I therefore ask for the honour of this dance?'

There was an audible gasp throughout the room. It wasn't said out loud but she could hear the thought regardless. *Who?*

But Ramón was holding out his hand, waiting for her to put hers in his. Smiling. It was the smile she loved with all her heart.

Was this how Cinders felt?

And then Cinders was forgotten. Everything was forgotten. She put her hand in his, she tried hard to smile back and she allowed the Crown Prince of Cepheus to lead her onto the ballroom floor.

Where had she learned to dance?

Ramón had been coached almost before he could walk. His grandmother had thought dancing at least as important as any other form of movement. He could thus waltz without thinking. He'd expected to slow his steps to Jenny's, to take care she wasn't embarrassed, but he'd been on the dance floor less than ten seconds before he realized such precautions weren't necessary. He took her into his arms in the waltz hold, and she melted into him as if she belonged.

The music swelled in an age-old, well-loved waltz and she was one with the music, one with him.

He'd almost forgotten how wonderful she felt.

He had to be formal, he told himself harshly. He needed to hold her at arm's length—which was difficult when he was not holding her at arm's length at all. He needed to be courteously friendly and he needed to thank her and say goodbye.

Only not yet. Not goodbye yet.

'Where did you learn to dance?' he managed, and it was a dumb thing to say to a woman after a three-month separation, but the tension eased a little and she almost smiled.

'Dancing's not reserved for royalty. My Papà was the best.'

This was better. There was small talk in this. 'He should have met my grandmother.'

'Yes,' she said, and seemed to decide to let herself enjoy the music, the dance, the sensation of being held for a couple more circuits of the floor while the world watched. And then… 'Ramón, why are you doing this?'

'I'm sorry?'

'Why did you ask me to dance…first?'

'I wanted to thank you.'

'You paid me, remember? It's me who should be thanking. And the world is watching. For you to ask me for the first dance…'

'I believe it's the last dance,' he said, and the leaden feeling settled back around his heart as the truth flooded back. Holding her was an illusion, a fleeting taste of what could have been, and all at once the pain was unbearable. 'I've wanted to hold you for three months,' he said simply, and it was as if the words were there and had to be said, whether he willed them or not. 'Jenny, maybe even saying it is unwise but, wise or not, I've missed you every single night.' He hesitated, then somehow struggled back to lightness, forcing the leaden ache to stay clear of his voice. He couldn't pass his regret onto her. He had to say goodbye—as friends. 'Do you realize how much work there is in being a Crown Prince?'

'I have no idea,' she said faintly. 'I guess…there's speeches to make. Ribbons to cut. That sort of thing.'

'Not so much of that sort of thing.' His hand tightened on her waist, tugging her closer. Wanting her closer. Sense decreed he had to let her go, but still not yet. 'I haven't even been official Crown Prince until today,' he said, fighting to make his voice sound normal. 'I've not even been qualified as a ribbon-cutter until now. I've been a prince in training. Nothing more. Nothing less. But I have been practising my waltzing. My Aunt Sofía's seen to that. So let's see if we can make the ghosts of your Papà and my Grand-mère proud?'

She smiled. He whirled her around in his arms and she felt like thistledown, he thought. She felt like Jenny.

He had to let her go.

He didn't feel like a prince, she thought as he held her close and their bodies moved as one. If she closed her eyes he felt like Ramón. Just Ramón, pure and simple. The man who'd stolen her heart.

It was impossible, he'd said. Of course it was. She'd known it for three months and nothing had changed.

The world was watching. She had to keep it light.

'So it's been practising speeches and waltzing,' she ventured at last. 'While we've been braving the Horn.'

'That and getting leggings to fit,' he murmured into her ear. 'Bloody things, leggings. I'd almost prefer the Horn.'

'But leggings are so sexy.'

'Sexy isn't leggings,' he said. His eyes were on her and she could see exactly what he was thinking.

'Don't,' she whispered, feeling her colour rising. Every eye in the room was on them.

'I've missed you for three long months,' he said, lightness disappearing. He sounded goaded almost past breaking point.

'Ramón, we had two weeks,' she managed. 'It didn't mean anything.'

He stopped dancing. Others had taken to the floor now, but they were on the edge of the dance floor. Ramón and Jenny had central position and they were still being watched.

'Are you saying what we had didn't mean anything to you?' he asked, his voice sounding suddenly calm, almost distant.

'Of course it did,' she said, blushing furiously. 'At the time. Ramón, please, can we keep dancing? I don't belong here.'

'Neither do I,' he said grimly, and he took her in his arms again and slipped back into the waltz. 'I should be leaving for Bangladesh right now. My team's left without me for the first time in years.'

'Speeches are important,' she said cautiously.

'They are.' The laughter and passion had completely disappeared now, leaving his voice sounding flat and defeated. 'Believe it or not, this country needs me. It's been bled dry by my grandfather and my uncle. If I walk away it'll continue to be bled dry by a government that's as corrupt as it is inept. It's not all ribbon-cutting.'

'It's your life,' she said simply. 'You're bred to it and you shouldn't be dancing with me.'

'I shouldn't be doing lots of things, and I'll not be told who I should be dancing with tonight. I know. This can only be for now *but I will dance with you tonight*.'

The music was coming to an end. The outside edge of the dance floor was crowded, but the dancers were keeping clear of the Crown Prince and his partner. A space was left so that, as soon as the dance ended, Ramón could return to his royal table.

Waiting for him were the crowned heads of Europe. Men and women who were watching Jenny as if they knew instinctively she had no place among them.

'You have danced with me,' Jenny said softly, disengaging her hands before he realized what she intended. 'I thank you for the honour.'

'There's no need to thank me.'

'Oh, but there is,' she said, breathless. 'The clothes, this moment, you. I'll remember it all my life.'

She looked up into his eyes and felt an almost overwhelming urge to reach up and kiss him, just a kiss, just a moment, to take a tiny taste of him to keep for ever. But the eyes of the world were on her. Ramón was a prince and his world was waiting.

'I believe there are women waiting to dance with the Crown Prince of Cepheus,' she murmured. 'We both need to move on, so thank you, Ramón. Thank you for the fantasy.'

'Thank you, Gianetta,' he murmured, and he raised his hand and touched her cheek, a feather touch that seemed a gesture of regret and loss and farewell. 'It's been my honour. I will see you before you leave.'

'Do you think…?'

'It's unwise? Of course it's unwise,' he finished for her. 'But it's tonight only. Tomorrow I need to be wise for the rest of my life.'

'Then maybe tomorrow needs to start now,' she said unsteadily and she managed a smile, her very best peasant to royalty smile, and turned and walked away. Leaving the Crown Prince of Cepheus looking after her.

What had he said? *'We can't take it further…'*

Of course they couldn't. What was she thinking of? But still she felt like sobbing. What was she doing here? Why had she ever come? She'd slip away like Gordon, she thought, just as soon as the next dance started, just as soon as everyone stopped watching her.

But someone was stepping into her path. Another prince? The man was dark and bold and so good-looking that if she hadn't met Ramón first she would have been stunned. As it was, she hardly saw him.

'May I request the honour of this dance?' he said, and it wasn't a question. His hand took hers before she could argue, autocratic as Ramón. Where did they learn this? Autocracy school?

It seemed no wasn't a word in these men's vocabularies. She was being led back onto the dance floor, like it or not.

'What's needed is a bit of spine,' she told herself and somehow she tilted her chin, fixed her smile and accepted partner after partner.

Most of these men were seriously good dancers. Many of these men were seriously good-looking men. She thought briefly of Cathy back in Seaport—*'Jenny, get a life!'* If Cathy could see her now…

The thought was almost enough to make her smile real. If only she wasn't so aware of the eyes watching her. If only she wasn't so aware of Ramón's presence. He was dancing with beautiful woman after beautiful woman, and a couple of truly impressive royal matriarchs as well.

He was smiling into each of his partner's eyes, and each one of them was responding exactly the same.

They melted.

Why would they not? Anyone would melt in Ramón's arms.

And suddenly, inexplicably, she was thinking of Matty, of her little son, and she wondered what she was doing here. This strange creature in fancy clothes had nothing to do with who she really was, and all at once what she was doing seemed a betrayal.

'It's okay,' she told herself, feeling suddenly desperate. 'This is simply an unbelievable moment out of my life. After tonight I'll return to being who I truly am. This is for one night only,' she promised Matty. 'One night and then I'm back where I belong.'

Her partner was holding her closer than was appropriate. Sadly for him, she was so caught up in her thoughts she hardly noticed.

Ramón was dancing so close that she could almost reach out and touch him. He whirled his partner round, his gaze caught hers and he smiled, and her partner had no chance at all.

That smile was so dangerous. That smile sucked you in.

'So who are your parents?' her partner asked, and she had to blink a few times to try and get her world moving again.

'My parents are dead,' she managed. 'And yours?'

'I beg your pardon?'

'Who are your parents?'

'My father is the King of Morotatia,' her partner said in stilted English. 'My mother was a princess in her own right before she married. And I am Prince Marcelo Pietros Cornelieus Maximus, heir to the throne of Morotatia.'

'That's wonderful,' she murmured. 'I guess you don't need to work for a living then?'

'Work?'

'I didn't think so,' she said sadly. 'But you guys must need muffins. I wonder if there's an opening around here for a kitchen maid.'

But, even as she said it, she knew even that wasn't possible. She had no place here. This was the fairy tale and she had to go home.

CHAPTER SEVEN

THE night was becoming oppressive. She was passed on to her next partner, who gently grilled her again, and then another who grilled her not so gently until she almost snapped at him. Finally supper was announced. She could escape now, she thought, but then a dumpy little lady with a truly magnificent tiara made a beeline for her, grasped her hands and introduced herself.

'I'm Ramón's Aunt Sofía. I'm so pleased to meet you.' She tucked her arm into Jenny's as if she was laying claim to her—as indeed she was, as there were those around them who were clearly waiting to start the inquisitions again.

'Aunt...'

Sofía turned to see Ramón approaching. He had one of the formidable matrons on his arm. Queen of somewhere? But Sofía was not impressed.

'Go away, Ramón,' Sofía commanded. 'I'm taking Jenny into supper. You look after Her Highness.'

'Sofía was always bossy,' the Queen of somewhere said, but she smiled, and Ramón gave his aunt a smile and gave Jenny a quick, fierce glance—one that was enough to make her toes curl—and led his queen away.

Sofía must rank pretty highly, Jenny thought, so dazed she simply allowed herself to be led. The crowd parted before them. Sofía led them to a small alcove set with a table and truly impressive tableware. She smiled at a passing servant and in two minutes there were so many delicacies before them Jenny could only gasp.

Sofía ate two bite-sized cream éclairs, then paused to demand why Jenny wasn't doing likewise.

'I'm rather in shock,' Jenny confessed.

'Me too,' Sofía confessed. 'And Ramón too, though we're making the best of it.'

'But Ramón's the Crown Prince,' Jenny managed. 'How can he be intimidated?' She could see him through the crowd. He drew every eye in the room. He looked truly magnificent—Crown Prince to the manor born.

'Because he wasn't meant to be royal,' Sofía said darkly, but then her darkness disappeared and she smiled encouragingly at Jenny. 'Just like you're not. I'm not sure what Ramón's told you so I thought maybe there's things you ought to know.'

'I know the succession was a shock,' Jenny ventured, and Sofía nodded vigorously and ate another éclair.

'Yes,' she said definitely. 'We were never expected to inherit. Ramón's grandfather—my father—sent my mother, my younger brother and I out of the palace when my brother and I were tiny. We were exiled, and kept virtual prisoners on an island just off the coast. My mother was never permitted to step back onto the mainland.'

Jenny frowned. Why was she being told this? But she could do nothing but listen as Sofía examined a meringue from all angles and decided not.

'That sounds dreadful,' Sofía continued, moving on to a delicate chocolate praline, popping it in and choosing another. 'But, in truth, the island is beautiful. It was only my mother's pain at what was happening to her country, and at losing her elder son that hurt. As we grew older my younger brother married an islander—a lovely girl. Ramón is their son. So Ramón's technically a prince, but until three months ago the only time he was at the palace was the night his father died.'

There were places here she didn't want to go. There were

places she had no right to go to. 'He…he spends his life on his yacht,' she ventured.

'No, dear, only part of it, and that's only since his mother and sister died. He trained as a builder. I think he started building things almost as soon as he could put one wooden block on top of another. He spends every dry season in Bangladesh, building houses with floating floors. Apparently they're brilliant—villagers can adjust their floor levels as flood water rises. He's passionate about it, but now, here he is, stuck as Crown Prince for ever.'

'I imagine he was trained for it,' Jenny said stiffly, still not sure where this was going.

'Only in that my mother insisted on teaching us court manners,' Sofía retorted. 'It was as if she knew that one day we'd be propelled back here. We humoured her, though none of us ever expected that we would. Finally, my brother tried to reinstate my mother's rights, to allow her to leave the island, and that's when the real tragedy started.'

'That was when Ramón's father was killed?'

'Yes, dear. By my father's thugs,' Sofía said, her plump face creasing into distress. The noise and bustle of the ballroom was nothing, ignored in her apparent need to tell Jenny this story. 'My mother ached to leave, and we couldn't believe my father's vindictiveness could last for years. But last it did, and when my brother was old enough he mounted a legal challenge. It was met with violence and with death. My father invited my brother here, to reason with him, so he came and brought Ramón with him because he thought he'd introduce his little son to his grandfather. So Ramón was here when it happened, a child, sleeping alone in this dreadful place while his father was killed. Just…alone.'

She stared down at her chocolate, but she wasn't seeing it. She was obviously still stunned at the enormity of what had happened. 'That's what royalty does,' she whispered. 'What is it they say? Absolute power corrupts absolutely. So my father had his own son killed, simply because he dared to defy him. We assume…we want to believe that it was simply his thugs going too far, meant to frighten but taking their orders past the point of reason. But still, my father must have employed them, and he must have known the consequences. This place…the whole of royalty is tainted by that murder. And now Carlos…the man who would have been Crown Prince if Ramón hadn't agreed to come home…is in the wings, threatening. He's here tonight.'

She gestured towards the supper table where a big man with more medals than Ramón was shovelling food into his mouth.

'He makes threats but so quietly we can't prove anything. He's here always, with his unfortunate wife towed in his wake, and he's just waiting for something to happen to Ramón. I can walk away—Ramón insists that I will walk away—but Ramón can't.'

Jenny was struggling to take everything in. She couldn't focus on shadows of death. She couldn't even begin to think of Carlos and his threats. She was still, in fact, struggling with genealogy. And Ramón as a little boy, alone as his father died…

'So…so the Crown Prince who's just been killed was your older brother?' she managed.

'Yes,' Sofía told her, becoming calm once more. 'Not that I ever saw him after we left the palace. And he had a son, who also had a son.' She shrugged. 'A little boy called Philippe. There's another tragedy. But it's not your tragedy, dear,' she said as she saw Jenny's face. 'Nor Ramón's. Ramón worries, but then Ramón worries about everything.' She hesitated, and then forged ahead as if this was something she'd rehearsed.

'But, my dear, Ramón's been talking about you,' she confessed. 'He says…he says you're special. Well, I can see that. I watched Ramón's face as he danced with you and it's exactly the same expression I saw on his father's face when he danced with his mother. If Ramón's found that with you…'

'He can't possibly…' Jenny started, startled, but Sofía was allowing no interruptions.

'You can't say it's impossible if it's already happened. All

I'm saying is that you don't have to be royal to be with Ramón. What I'm saying is give love a chance.'

'How could I…?' She stopped, bewildered.

'By not staying in this palace,' Sofía said, suddenly deadly serious. 'By not even thinking about it. Ramón's right when he tells me such a union is impossible, dangerous, unsuitable, and he can't be distracted from what he must do. You don't fit in and neither should you. Our real home, our lovely island, is less than fifteen minutes' helicopter ride from here. If Ramón could settle you there as his mistress, he'd have an escape.'

'An escape?' she whispered, stunned.

'From royalty,' Sofía said bluntly. 'Ramón needs to do his duty but if he could have you on the side…' She laid a hand over Jenny's. 'It could make all the difference. And he'd look after you so well. I know he would. You'd want for nothing. So, my dear, will you listen to Ramón?'

'If he asks…to have me as his some-time mistress?' she managed.

'I'm just letting you know his family would think it was a good thing,' Sofía said, refusing to be deterred by Jenny's obvious shock. 'You're not to take offence, but it's nothing less than my duty to tell you that you're totally unsuitable for this place, even if he'd have you here, which he won't. You're not who Ramón needs as a wife. He needs someone who knows what royalty is and how to handle it. That's what royal pedigree is—there's a reason for it. But, as for a partner he loves…that's a different thing. If Ramón could have you now and then…'

She paused, finally beginning to flounder. The expression on Jenny's face wasn't exactly encouraging. She was finding it impossible to contain her anger, and her humiliation.

'So you'd have him marry someone else and have me on the side,' she said dangerously.

'It's been done for generation upon generation,' Sofía said with asperity. Then she glanced up with some relief as a stranger approached, a youngish man wearing more medals than Ramón. 'But here's Lord Anthony, wanting an introduction. He's frightfully British, my dear, but he's a wonderful dancer. Ramón won't have any more time for you tonight. He'll have so little time... But I'm sure he could fit you in every now and then, if you'll agree to the island. So you go and dance with Lord Anthony, and remember what I said when you need to remember it.'

Jenny danced almost on automatic pilot. She desperately wanted to leave, but slipping away when the world was watching was impossible. As Sofía had warned her, she barely saw Ramón again. He was doing his duty, dancing with one society dame after another.

She'd been lucky to be squeezed in at all, she thought dully. What *was* she doing here?

It wasn't made better with her second 'girls' talk' of the night. Another woman grabbed her attention almost straight after Sofía. This lady was of a similar age to Sofía, but she was small and thin, she had fewer jewels and she had the air of a frightened rabbit. But she was a determined frightened rabbit. She intercepted Jenny between partners. When the next man approached she hissed, 'Go away,' and stood her ground until they were left alone.

'I'm Perpetua,' she said, and then, as Jenny looked blank, she explained. 'I'm Carlos's wife.'

Carlos. The threat.

'He's not dangerous,' Perpetua said, obviously reading her expression, and she steered her into the shadows with an air of quiet but desperate determination. 'My husband's all talk. All stupidity. It's this place. It's being royal. I just wanted to say...to say...'

She took a deep breath and out it came, as if it had been welled up for years. 'They say you're common,' she said. 'I mean...ordinary. Not royal. Like me. I was a schoolteacher, and I loved my work and then I met Carlos. For a while we were happy, but then the old Prince decided he liked my husband. He used to take him gambling. Carlos got sucked into the lifestyle, and that's where he stays. In some sort of fantasy world, where he's more royal than Ramón. He's done some really stupid things, most of them at the Prince's goading. In these last months when he thought he would inherit the throne, he's been…a little bit crazy. There's nothing I can do, but it's so painful to see the way he is, the way he's acting. And then I watched you tonight. The way you looked at Ramón when you were dancing.'

'I don't understand,' Jenny managed.

'Just get away from it,' she whispered. 'Whatever Ramón says, don't believe it. Just run. Oh, I shouldn't say anything. I'm a royal wife and a royal wife just shuts up. Do you want that? To be an appendage who just shuts up? My dear, don't do it. Just run.' And then, as yet another potential partner came to claim Jenny's hand, she gave a gasping sob, shot Jenny one last despairing glance and disappeared into the crowd.

Just run. That was truly excellent advice, Jenny thought, as she danced on, on autopilot. It was the best advice she'd had all night. If she knew where she was, if she knew how to get back to the boat in the dark in the middle of a strange city, that was just what she'd do.

She'd never felt so alone. She was Cinderella without her coach and it wasn't even midnight.

But finally the clock struck twelve. Right on cue, a cluster of officials gathered round Ramón as a formal guard of honour. Trumpets blared with a final farewell salute, and the Crown Prince Ramón of Cepheus was escorted away.

He'd be led to his harem of nubile young virgins, Jenny decided, fighting back an almost hysterical desire to laugh. Or cry. Or both. She was so weary she wanted to sink and, as if the thought had been said aloud, a footman was at her side, courteously solicitous.

'Ma'am, I'm to ask if you'd like to stay on to continue dancing, or would you like to be escorted back to your chambers?'

'I'd like to be escorted back to the yacht.'

'That's not possible, ma'am,' he said. 'The Prince's orders are that you stay in the palace.' And then, as she opened her mouth to argue, he added flatly, 'There's no transport to the docks tonight. I'm sorry, ma'am, but you'll have to stay.'

So that, it seemed, was that. She was escorted back to the palace. She lay in her ridiculously ostentatious bedchamber, in her ridiculously ostentatious bed, and she tried for sleep.

How was a girl to sleep after a night like this?

She couldn't. Her crimson ball-gown was draped on a hanger in the massive walk-in wardrobe. The diamond necklet still lay on her dresser. Her Cinderella slippers were on the floor beside her bed.

At least she'd kept both of them on, she thought ruefully. It hadn't quite been a fairy tale.

Only it had been a fairy tale. Gianetta Bertin—Jenny to her friends—had attended a royal ball. She'd been led out onto the dance floor with a prince so handsome he made her knees turn to jelly. For those few wonderful moments she'd let herself be swept away into a magic future where practicalities disappeared and there was only Ramón; only her love.

And then his aunt had told her that she was totally un-suitable to be a royal wife but she could possibly be his mistress. Only not here. How romantic.

And then someone called Perpetua had warned her against royalty, like the voice of doom in some Gothic novel. *Do not trust him, gentle maiden.*

How ridiculous.

And, as if in response to her unanswerable question, some-one knocked on the door.

Who'd knock on her bedroom door at three in the morning?

'Who is it?' she quavered, and her heart seemed to stop until there was a response.

'I can't get my boots off,' a beloved voice complained from the other side of the door. 'I was hoping someone might hang on while I pull.'

'I… I believe my contract was all about muffins and sails,' she managed, trying to make her voice not squeak, trying to kick-start her heart again while warnings and sensible decisions went right out of the window. *Ramón.*

'I know I have no right to ask.' There was suddenly seriousness behind Ramón's words. 'I know this isn't sensible, I know I shouldn't be here, but Jenny, if tonight is all there is then I'm sure, if we read the contract carefully, there might be something about boots. Something that'd give us an excuse for…well, something about helping me for this night only.'

'Don't you have a valet?' she whispered and then wondered how he'd hear her through the door. But it was as if he was already in the room with her.

'Valets scare the daylights out of me,' he said. 'They're better dressed than I am. Please, Jenny love, will you help me off with my boots?'

'I don't think I'm brave enough.'

'You helped a trapped whale. Surely you can help a trapped prince. For this night only.'

'Ramón…'

'Open the door, Gianetta,' he said in a different voice, a voice that had her flinging back her bedcovers and flying to the door and tugging it open. Despite what Sofía had said, despite Perpetua's grim warnings, this was Ramón. Her Ramón.

And there he was. He wasn't smiling. He was just…him.

He opened his arms and she walked right in.

For a long moment she simply stood, held against him, feeling the strength of his heartbeat, feeling his arms around her. He was still in his princely uniform. There were medals digging into her cheek but she wasn't complaining. His heart was beating right under those medals, and who cared about a bit of metal anyway?

Who cared what two royal women had said to her? Who cared that this was impossible?

They had this night.

He kissed the top of her head and he held her tight and she felt protected and loved—and desperate to haul him into the room right there and then.

But there was a footman at the top of the stairs. Just standing, staring woodenly ahead. He was wigged, powdered, almost a dummy. But he was real.

It was hard to seize a prince and haul him into her lair when a footman was on guard.

'Um…we have an audience,' she whispered at last.

He kissed her hair again and said gravely, 'Do you care?'

'If we walk into my room and shut the door we won't have an audience,' she tried.

'Ah, but the story will out,' he said gravely.

'So it should if you go creeping into strange women's bedrooms in the small hours. I should yell the house down.'

She was trying to sound indignant. She was trying to pull back so she could be at arm's length, so she could see his face. She wasn't trying hard enough. She sounded happy—and there was no way she was pulling back from this man.

'You could if you wanted and you'd have help,' he said gravely. 'The footman's on guard duty. In case the Huns invade—or strange women don't want strange men doing this creeping thing you describe. But if the woman was to welcome this strange man, then we don't need an audience. Gianetta, are you hungry?'

Hungry. The thought was so out of left field that she blinked.

'Hungry?'

'I'm starving. I was hoping you might come down to the kitchen with me.'

'After I've pulled your boots off?'

'Yup.'

'You want me to be your servant?'

'No,' he said, lightness giving way instantly to a gravity she found disconcerting. 'For this night, I want you to be my friend.'

Her friend, the prince?

Her friend, her lover?

Ramón.

Part-time mistress?

Forget Sofía, she told herself fiercely. Forget Perpetua. Tonight she'd hold on to the fairy tale.

'So…so there's no royal cook?' she managed.

'There are three, but they scare me more than my valet. They wear white hats and speak with Italian accents and say béchamel a lot.'

'Oh, Ramón…'

'And there's no security camera in the smaller kitchen,' he told her, and she looked up into his face and it was all she could do not to burst into spontaneous combustion.

'So will you come?' His eyes dared her.

'I'm coming.' Mistress or not, dangerous or not, right now she'd take whatever he wanted to give. Stupid? Who knew? She only knew that there was no way she could walk away from this man this night.

'Slippers and robe first,' he suggested and she blinked.

'Pardon?'

'Let's keep it nice past the footman.' He grinned. 'And do your belt up really tight. I like a challenge.'

'Ramón…'

'Second kitchen, no security camera,' he said and gave her a gentle push back into her bedroom. 'Slippers and gown. Respectability's the thing, my love. All the way down the stairs.'

They were respectable all the way down the stairs. The footman watched them go, his face impassive. When they reached the second kitchen another footman appeared and opened the door for them. He ushered them inside.

'Would you like the door closed?' he said deferentially and Ramón nodded.

'Absolutely. And make sure the Huns stay on that side.'

'The Huns?' the man said blankly.

'You never know what they're planning,' Ramón said darkly. 'If I were you, I'd take a walk around the perimeter of the palace. Warn the troops.'

'Your Highness…'

'Just give us a bit of privacy,' Ramón said, relenting at the look of confusion on the man's face. 'Fifty paces from the kitchen door, agreed?'

Finally there was a smile—sort of—pulled back instantly with a gasp as if the man had realized what he was doing and maybe smiling was a hanging offence. Impassive again, he snapped his heels and moved away and Ramón closed the door and leaned on it.

'This servant thing's got knobs on it. Three months and they still treat me like a prince.'

'You are a prince.'

'Not here,' he said. 'Not now. I'm me and you're you and the kitchen door is closed. And so…'

And so he took her into his arms and he held her so tight the breath was crushed from her body. He held her like a man drowning holding on to a lifeline. He held her and held her and held her, as if there was no way he could ever let her go.

He didn't kiss her. His head rested on her hair. He held her until her heart beat in synchronisation with his. Until she felt as if her body was merging with his, becoming one. Until she felt as if she was truly loved—that she'd come home.

How long they stayed there she could never afterwards tell—time disappeared. This was their moment. The world was somewhere outside that kitchen door, the servants, Sofía's words, Perpetua's warnings, tomorrow, but for now all that mattered was this, her Ramón. Her love.

The kitchen was warm. An old fire-stove sent out a gentle heat. A small grey cat slept in a basket by the hearth. All Jenny had seen of this palace was grandeur, but here in this second kitchen the palace almost seemed a home.

It did feel like home. Ramón was holding her against his heart and she was where she truly belonged.

She knew it was an illusion, and so must he. Maybe that was why he held her for so long, allowing nothing, no words, no movement, to intrude. As if, by holding her, the world could be kept at bay. As if she was something that he must lose, but he'd hold on while he still could.

Finally he kissed her as she needed to be kissed, as she ached to be kissed, and she kissed him back as if he was truly her Ramón and the royal title was nothing but a crazy fantasy locked securely on the other side of the door.

With the Huns, she thought, somewhat deliriously. Reality and the Huns were being kept at bay by powdered, wigged footmen, giving her this time of peace and love and bliss.

She loved this man with all her heart. Maybe what Sofía had said was wrong. Maybe the Perpetua thing was crazy.

The cat stirred, coiling out of her basket, stretching, then stepping daintily out to inspect her food dish. The tiny movement was enough to make them stir, to let a sliver of reality in. But only a sliver.

'She's only interested in her food,' Jenny whispered. 'Not us.'

'I don't blame her. I'm hungry, too.' Ramón's voice was husky with passion, but his words were so prosaic that she chuckled. It made it real. Her Prince of the Blood, dressed in medals and tassels and boots that shone like mirrors, was smiling down at her with a smile that spoke of devilry and pure latent sex—and he was hungry.

'For…for what?' she managed, and the devilry in his eyes darkened, gleamed, sprang into laughter.

'I'd take you on the kitchen table, my love,' he said simply. 'But I just don't trust the servants that much.'

'And we'd shock the cat,' she whispered and he chuckled. 'Absolutely.'

He was trying to make his voice normal, Jenny thought. He was trying to make their world somehow normal. In truth, if Ramón carried out his earlier threat to untie the cord of her dressing gown, if he took that to its inevitable conclusion, there was no way she'd deny him. Only sense was prevailing. Sort of.

Where he led, she'd follow, but if he was trying to be prosaic…maybe she could be, too.

'I could cook in this kitchen,' she said, eyeing the old range appraisingly, the rows of pots and pans hanging from overhead rails, the massive wooden table, worn and pitted from years of scrubbing.

'The pantry adjoins both kitchens,' Ramón said hopefully. 'I'm sure there's eggs and bacon in there.'

'Are you really hungry?'

'At dinner I had two queens, one duke and three prime ministers within talking range,' he said. 'They took turns to address me. It's very rude for a Crown Prince to eat while being addressed by a Head of State. My Aunt Sofía was watching. If I'd eaten I would have had my knuckles rapped.'

'She's a terrifying lady,' Jenny said and he grinned.

'I love her to bits,' he said simply. 'Like I love you.'

'Ramón…'

'Gianetta.'

'This is…'

'Just for tonight,' he said softly and his voice grew bleak. 'I know this is impossible. After tonight I'll ask nothing of you, but Gianetta…just for tonight can we be…us?'

His face was grim. There were vast problems here, she knew, and she saw those problems reflected in his eyes. Sofía had said the ghost of his father made this palace hateful, yet Ramón was stuck here.

Can we be us?

Maybe they could go back to where they' started.

'Do you want bacon and eggs, or do you want muffins?' she asked and tried to make her voice prosaic.

'You could cook muffins here?' Astonishment lessened the grimness.

'You have an oven warmed for a cat,' she said. 'It seems silly to waste it. It'll mean you need to wait twenty minutes instead of five minutes for eggs and bacon.'

'And the smell will go all through the palace,' he said in satisfaction. 'There's an alibi if ever I heard one. We could give a couple to Manuel and Luis.'

'Manuel and Luis?'

'Our Hun protectors. They think I'm taunting them if I use their real names, but surely a muffin couldn't be seen as a taunt.' His eyes were not leaving hers. He wanted her. He ached for her. His eyes said it all, but he was keeping himself rigidly under control.

'You think we might find the ingredients?' he asked, but she was already opening the panty door, doing a visual sweep of the shelves, then checking out the first of three massive refrigerators. As anxious as he to find some way of keeping the sizzle between them under control, and to keep the tension on his face at bay.

'There's more ingredients than you can shake a stick at.'

'Pardon?'

'Lots of ingredients,' she said in satisfaction. 'It seems a shame to abandon bacon entirely. You want bacon and cheese muffins, or double chocolate chip?'

'Both,' he said promptly. 'Especially if I get to lick the chocolate chip bowl.'

'Done,' she said and smiled at him and his smile met hers and she thought, whoa I am in such trouble. And then she thought, whatever Sofía said, or Perpetua said, no matter how impossible this is, I'm so deeply in love, there's no way I'll ever be able to climb out.

CHAPTER EIGHT

THEY made muffins. Not just half a dozen muffins because: 'If I'm helping, it's not such a huge ask to make heaps,' Ramón declared. 'We can put them on for breakfast and show the world what my Gianetta can do.'

'You'll upset the chefs,' Jenny warned.

'If there's a turf war, you win hands down.'

'A turf war...' She was pouring choc chips into her mixture but she hesitated at that. 'I'm not interested in any turf war. Frankly, this set-up leaves me terrified.'

'It leaves me terrified.'

'Yes, but...'

'But I have no choice,' he said flatly, finishing the sentence for her. 'I know that. In the good old days, as Crown Prince I could have simply had my soldiers go out with clubs and drag you to my lair.'

'And now you give me choices,' she retorted, trying desperately to keep things light, whisking her muffin mix more briskly than she needed. 'Just as well. I believe clubbing might create an International Incident.'

'I miss the good old days,' he said morosely. He was sitting on the edge of the table, swinging his gorgeous boots, taking taste tests of her mixture. So sexy the kitchen seemed to sizzle. 'What use is being a prince if I can't get my woman?'

My woman. She was dreaming, Jenny thought dreamily. She was cooking muffins for her prince.

My woman?

She started spooning her mixture into the pans and Ramón reached over and took the trays and the bowl from her. 'I can do this,' he said. 'If you do something for me.'

'What?'

'Pull my boots off. I asked you ages ago.'

'I thought you were kidding.'

'They're killing me,' he confessed. 'I've spent my life in either boat shoes, bare feet or steel-toed construction boots. These make me feel like my feet are in corsets and I can't get them off. Please, dear, kind Jenny, will you pull my boots off?'

He was sitting on the table. He was spooning muffin mixture into pans. He was holding his boots out for her to pull.

This was so ridiculous she couldn't help giggling.

She wiped her hands—it'd be a pity to get chocolate on leather like this—took position, took a boot in both hands—and pulled.

The boot didn't budge. It was like a second skin.

'See what I mean,' Ramón said morosely. 'And I really don't want to wake a valet. You think I should cut them off?'

'You can't cut them,' Jenny said, shocked, and tried again. The boot budged, just a little.

'Hey,' Ramón said, continuing to spoon. 'It's coming.'

'I'll pull you off the table if I tug any harder,' Jenny warned.

'I'm strong,' he said, too smugly, keeping on spooning. 'My balance is assured.'

'Right,' she said and glowered, reacting to his smugness. She wiped both her hands on her dressing gown, took the boot in both hands, took a deep breath—and pulled like she'd never pulled.

The boot held, gripped for a nano-second and then gave. Jenny lurched backward, boot in hand, lost her balance and fell backwards.

Ramón slid off the table, staggered—and ended up on the floor.

The half-full bowl slid off after him, tipped sideways and mixture oozed out over the floor.

Jenny stared across at him in shock. Ramón stared back at her—her lovely prince, half bootless, sprawled on the floor, surrounded by choc chip muffin mixture.

Her Ramón.

She couldn't help it. She laughed out loud, and it was a magical release of tension, a declaration of love and happiness if ever there was one, and she couldn't help what happened next either. It was as if restraint had been thrown to the wind and she could do what she liked—and there was no doubting what she'd like. She slid over the floor, she took Ramón's face in both her hands—and she kissed him.

And Ramón kissed her back—a thoroughly befuddled, laughing, wonderful kiss. He tasted of choc chip muffin. He tasted of love.

He tugged her close, hauling her backward with him so she was in his arms, and they were so close she thought she must…they must…

And then the door burst open and Sofía was standing in the doorway staring at them both as if they'd lost their minds.

Maybe they had.

The little cat was delicately licking muffin mixture from the floor. Sofía darted across and retrieved the cat as if she were saving her from poison.

'Hi, Sofía,' Ramón said innocently from somewhere underneath his woman. Jenny would have pulled away but he was having none of it. He tugged her close and held, so they were lying on the floor like two children caught out in mischief. Or more.

Sofía stared down at them as if she couldn't believe her eyes. 'What do you think you're doing?' she hissed.

'Making muffins, Ramón said, and he would have pulled Jenny closer but the mixture of confusion and distress on Sofía's face was enough to have her pulling away. The timer was buzzing. Somehow she struggled to her feet. She opened the oven and retrieved her now cooked bacon muffins. Then she thought what the heck, she might as well finish what she'd started, so she put the almost full tray of choc chip muffins in to replace them.

'Gianetta's a professional,' Ramón said proudly to his aunt, struggling up as well. 'I told you she was fabulous.'

'Are you out of your minds?'

'No, I…'

'You're just like the rest,' she hissed at him. 'They're all womanisers, all the men who've ever held power here. You have her trapped. Ramón, what on earth is it that you're planning?'

'I'm not planning anything.'

'If it's marriage… You can't. I know Philippe needs a mother but this is…'

'It's nothing to do with Philippe,' Ramón snapped. 'Why are you here?'

'Why do you think?' Sofía's anger was becoming almost apoplectic. 'Did you think the two of you were invisible? Everyone knows where you are. Ramón, think about what you're doing. You're no longer just responsible for yourself. You represent a country now! She's a nice girl, I won't let you ruin her, or trap her into this life.'

'I won't do either,' Ramón said, coldly furious. 'We're not talking marriage. We're not talking anything past this night. Jenny will be leaving…'

'Ramón, if she goes to the island now… There'll be such talk. To take her in the palace kitchen…'

'He didn't *take* me…' It was Jenny's turn to be angry now. 'My dressing gown cord's still done up.'

'No one can tell that from outside,' Sofía snapped and walked across and tugged the door wide. 'See? The harm's done,' she said, as two footmen stepped smartly away from the door.

'You can't be happy here,' she whispered. 'No one knows anyone. No one trusts.'

'I know that,' Ramón told her. 'Sofía, stop this.'

'I told her you should take her to the island. I told her. You should have waited.'

'Excuse me?' Jenny said. 'Can you include me in this?'

'It's nothing to do with you,' Sofía said and then seemed to think about it. Her anger faded and she suddenly sounded weary and defeated. 'No. I mean…even if you were suitable as a royal bride—which you aren't—you aren't tough enough. To do it with no training…'

'Sofía, don't do this,' Ramón said. Sofía's distress was clear and real. 'We aren't talking about marriage.'

'Then you're ruining her for nothing. And here's your valet, come to see what all the fuss is about.'

'I don't want my valet,' Ramón snapped. 'I don't want any valet.'

'You don't have a choice,' Sofía said with exasperation. 'None of us do. Ramón, go away. I'll stay here with Jenny until these…whatever you're making…muffins?…are cooked. We'll make the best of a bad situation but there's no way we can keep this quiet. This, with your stupid insistence on dancing with her first tonight… She'll have paparazzi in her face tomorrow, whether she leaves or not.'

'Paparazzi…' Jenny said faintly.

'Leave now, Ramón, and don't go near her again. She needs space to see what a mess this situation is.'

'She doesn't want space.'

'Yes, I do,' Jenny said. Philippe? Paparazzi? There were so many unknowns. What was she getting into?

She felt dizzy.

She felt bereft.

'Jenny,' Ramón said urgently but Sofía was before him, pushing herself between them.

'Leave it,' she told them both harshly. 'Like it or not, Ramón is Crown Prince. He needs to fit his new role. He might think he wants you but he doesn't have a choice. *You* don't belong in our world and you both know it.' She glanced along the corridor where there were now four servants waiting. 'So… There's to be no seduction tonight. We're all calmly eating muffins and going to bed. Yes?'

'Yes,' Jenny said before Ramón could reply. She didn't

want to look at him. She couldn't. Because the laughter in his eyes had gone.

The servants were waiting to take over. The palace was waiting to take over.

She lay in her opulent bed and her head spun so much she felt dizzy.

She was lying on silk sheets. When she moved, she felt as if she was being caressed.

She wasn't being caressed. She was lying in a royal bed, in a royal boudoir. Alone. Because why?

Because Ramón was a Crown Prince.

Even when she'd lain with him in his wonderful yacht, believing he was simply the skipper and not the owner, she'd felt a sense of inequality, as if this couldn't be happening to her.

But it had happened, and now it was over.

What else had she expected?

Since she'd met Ramón her ache of grief had lifted. Life had become…unreal. But here it was again, reality, hard and cold as ice, slamming her back to earth. Grief was real. Loss was real. Emptiness and heartache had been her world for years, and here they were again.

Her time with Ramón, her time tonight, had been some sort of crazy soap bubble. Even before Sofía had spelled it out, she'd known it was impossible.

Sofía said she was totally unsuitable. Of course she was. But…but…

As the night wore on something strange was happening. Her grief for Matty had been in abeyance during the two weeks with Ramón, and again tonight. It was back with her now, but things had changed. Things were changing.

Ever since Matty was born, things had happened to Jenny. Just happened. It was as if his birth, his medical problems, his desperate need, had put her on a roller coaster of emotions that she couldn't get off. Her life was simply doing what came next.

But the chain of events today had somehow changed

things. What Sofía and then Perpetua had said had stirred something deep within. Or maybe it was how Ramón had made her feel tonight that was making her feel different.

She'd seen the defeat on Ramón's face and she recognized that defeat. It was a defeat born of bleak acceptance.

Once upon a time she'd shared it. Maybe she still should. But…but…

'Why should I run?' she whispered and she wondered if she'd really said it.

It didn't make any sense. Sofía and Perpetua were right. So was Ramón. What was between them was clearly impossible, and there'd be a million more complications she hadn't thought of yet.

Philippe? The child Sofía had talked of?

She didn't go near children. Not after Matty.

And royalty? She had no concept of what Ramón was facing. Threats? The unknown Carlos?

There were questions everywhere, unspoken shadows looming from all sides, but overriding everything was the fact that she wanted Ramón so much she could almost cry out loud for him. What she wanted right now was to pad out into the palace corridor, yell at the top of her lungs for Ramón and then sit down and demand answers.

She'd had her chance. She'd used it making muffins. And kissing her prince.

He'd kissed her back.

The memory made her smile. Ramón made her smile.

Maybe the shadows weren't so long, she thought, but she knew they were.

'I'd be happy as his lover,' she whispered to the night. 'For as long as he wanted me. Just as his lover. Just in private. Back on his boat, sailing round the world, Ramón and me.'

It wasn't going to happen. And would she be happy on his island, being paid occasional visits as Sofía had suggested?

No!

She lay back on her mound of feather pillows and she stared up at the ceiling some more.

She stared at nothing.

Jenny and Ramón, the Crown Prince of Cepheus? No and no and no.

But still there was this niggle. It wasn't anger, exactly. Not exactly.

It was more that she'd found her centre again.

She'd found something worth fighting for.

Gianetta and the Crown Prince of Cepheus? No and no and no.

The thing was, though, sense had gone out of the window.

The car crash that had killed his mother and his sister had left him with an aching void where family used to be. For years he'd carried the grief as a burden, thinking he could bear no more, and the way to avoid that was to not let people close.

He loved his work in Bangladesh—it changed people's lives—yet individual lives were not permitted to touch him.

But there was something about Jenny…Gianetta…that broke the barriers he'd built. She'd touched a chord, and the resonance was so deep and so real that to walk away from her seemed unthinkable.

For the last three months he'd tried to tell himself what he'd felt was an illusion, but the moment he'd seen her again he'd known it was real. She was his woman. He knew it with a certainty so deep it felt primeval.

But to drag her into the royal limelight, into a place where the servants greeted you with blank faces…into a place where his father had died and barely a ripple had been created…where Carlos threatened and he didn't know which servants might be loyal and which might be in Carlos's pay… here his duty lay to his people and to have his worry centred on one slip of a girl…

On Jenny.

No.

Could he love her enough to let her go?

He must.

He had a deputation from neighbouring countries meeting

him first thing in the morning to discuss border issues. Refugees. The thought did his head in.

Royalty seemed simple on the outside—what had Jenny said?—cutting ribbons and making speeches. But Cepheus was governed by royalty. He'd set moves afoot to turn it into a democracy but it would take years, and meanwhile what he did would change people's lives.

Could he do it alone? He must.

He had no right to ask Jenny to share a load he found insupportable. To put her into the royal limelight... To ask her to share the risks that had killed his father... To distract himself from a task that had to be faced alone...

There was no choice at all.

CHAPTER NINE

JENNY didn't see Ramón all the next day. She couldn't. 'Affairs of State,' Sofía told her darkly, deeply disapproving when Jenny told her she had no intention of leaving until she'd spoken to Ramón. 'There's so much business that's been waiting for Ramón to officially take charge. Señor Rodriguez tells me he's booked for weeks. Poor baby.'

Poor baby? Jenny thought of the man whose boot she'd pulled off, she thought of the power of his touch, and she thought 'poor baby' was a description just a wee bit wide of the mark.

So what was she to do? By nine she'd breakfasted, inspected the palace gardens—breathtakingly beautiful but *so* empty—got lost twice in the palace corridors, and she was starting to feel as if she was climbing walls.

She headed out to the gardens again and found Gordon, pacing by one of the lagoon-sized swimming pools. It seemed the darkness and the strange city last night had defeated even him.

'All this opulence gives me the creeps,' he said, greeting her with relief. 'I've been waiting for you. How about if we slope off down to the docks? It's not so far. A mile or so as the crow flies. We could get out the back way, avoid the paparazzi.'

'I do need to come back,' she whispered, looking at the cluster of cameramen around the main gate with dismay, and Gordon surveyed her with care.

'Are you sure? There's talk, lass, about last night.'

And there it was again, that surge of anger.

'Then maybe I need to give them something to talk about,' she snapped.

The meetings were interminable—men and women in serious suits, with serious briefcases filled with papers covered with serious concerns, not one of which he could walk away from.

This country had been in trouble for decades—was still in trouble. It would take skill and commitment to bring it back from the brink, to stop the exodus of youth leaving the country, to take advantage of the country's natural resources to bring prosperity for citizens who'd been ignored for far too long.

The last three months he'd spent researching, researching, researching. He had the knowledge now to make a difference, but so much work was before him it felt overwhelming.

He should be gearing up right now to spend the next six months supervising the construction of houses in Bangladesh, simple work but deeply satisfying. He'd had to abandon that to commit to this, a more direct and personal need.

And this morning he'd had to abandon Jenny.

Gianetta.

The two words kept interplaying in his head. Jenny. Gianetta.

Jenny was the woman who made muffins, the woman who saved whales, the woman who made him laugh.

Gianetta was the woman he took to his bed. Gianetta was the woman he would make his Princess—*if* he didn't care so much, for her and for his country.

Where was she now?

He'd been wrong last night. Sofía had spelled out their situation clearly and he could do nothing but agree.

He should be with her now, explaining why he couldn't take things further. She'd be confused and distressed. But there was simply no option for him to spend time with her today.

So... He'd left orders for her to be left to enjoy a day of leisure. The *Marquita* was a big boat; it was hard work to crew her and she'd been sailing for three months. Last night had been...stressful. She deserved to rest.

He had meetings all day and a formal dinner tonight. Tomorrow, though, he'd make time early to say goodbye. If she stayed that long.

And tomorrow he'd promised to visit Philippe.

He glanced at his watch. Tomorrow. It was twenty-two hours and thirty minutes before a scheduled visit with his woman. Wedging it in between affairs of state and his concern for a child he didn't know what to do with.

Jenny. How could he ever make sense of what he felt for her?

He knew, in his heart, that he couldn't.

The *Marquita* meant work, and in work there was respite.

The day was windless so they could unfurl the sails and let them dry. The boat was clean, but by common consensus they decided it wasn't clean enough. They scrubbed the decks, they polished brass, they gave the interior such a clean that Martha Gardener would be proud of them.

Jenny remade the bed in the great stateroom, plumped the mass of pillows, looked down at the sumptuous quilts and wondered again, what had she been thinking?

She'd slept in this bed with the man she loved. She loved him still, with all her heart, but in the distance she could see the spires of the palace, glistening white in the Mediterranean sunshine.

The Crown Prince of Cepheus. For a tiny time their two disparate worlds had collided, and they'd seemed almost equal. Now, all that was left was to find the courage to walk away.

Perhaps.

Eighteen hours and twenty-two minutes. How many suits could he talk to in that time? How many documents must he read?

He had to sign them all and there was no way he could sign without reading.

His eyes were starting to cross.

Eighteen hours and seven minutes.

Would she still be here?

Surely she wouldn't leave without a farewell.

He deserved it, he thought, but please…no.

They worked solidly until mid-afternoon. Gordon was checking the storerooms, taking inventory, making lists of what needed to be replaced. Jenny was still obsessively cleaning.

Taking away every trace of her.

But, as the afternoon wore on, even she ran out of things to do. 'Time to get back to the palace,' Gordon decreed.

'We could stay on board.'

'She's being pulled out of the water tonight so engineers can check her hull in the morning. We hardly have a choice tonight.'

'Will you stay on as Ramón's skipper?'

'I love this boat,' he said simply. 'For as long as I'm asked, I'll stay. If that means staying at the palace from time to time, I'll find the courage.'

'I don't have very much courage,' she whispered.

'Or maybe you have sense instead,' Gordon said stoutly. He stood back for her to precede him up to the deck. She stepped up—and suddenly the world was waiting for her.

Paparazzi were everywhere. Flashlights went off in her face, practically blinding her. She put her hand over her eyes in an instinctive gesture of defence, and retreated straight back down again.

Gordon slammed the hatch after her.

'Tell us about yourself,' someone called from the dock. 'You speak Spanish, right?'

'We're happy to pay for your story,' someone else called.

'You and Prince Ramón were on the boat together for two weeks, alone, right?' That was bad enough. But then…

'Is it true you had a baby out of wedlock?' someone else called while Jenny froze. 'And the baby died?'

They knew about her Matty? They knew....

She wanted to go home right now. She wanted to creep into a bunk and stay hidden while Gordon sailed her out of the harbour and away.

Serenity. Peace. That was what she'd been striving for since Matty died. Where was serenity and peace now?

How could she find it in this?

'I'll talk to them,' Gordon said, looking stunned and sick, and she looked at this big shy man and she thought why should he fight her battles? Why should anyone fight her battles?

Maybe she had to fight to achieve this so-called serenity, she thought. Maybe that was what her problem had been all along. She'd been waiting for serenity to find her, when all along it was something she needed to fight for.

Or maybe it wasn't even serenity that she wanted.

Then, before she had time to decide she'd lost her mind entirely—for maybe she had; she certainly wasn't making sense to herself and Gordon was looking really worried—she flung open the hatch again and stepped out onto the deck.

His cellphone was on mute in his pocket. He felt it vibrate, checked it and saw it was Gordon calling. Gordon wouldn't call him except in an emergency.

The documents had just been signed and the Heads of State were lining up for a photo call. These men had come for the coronation and had stayed on.

Cepheus was a small nation. These men represented far more powerful nations than his, and Cepheus had need of powerful allies. Nevertheless, he excused himself and answered.

'Paparazzi know about Jenny's baby,' Gordon barked, so loud he almost burst Ramón's eardrum. 'They're on the jetty. We're surrounded. You need to get her out of here.'

He felt sick. 'I'll have a security contingent there in two

minutes,' he said, motioning to Señor Rodriguez, who, no doubt, had heard every word. 'I need to get to the docks,' he told him. 'How long?'

'It would take us fifteen minutes, Your Highness, but we can't leave here,' Rodriguez said. The man was seriously good. He already had security on his second phone. 'Security will have dealt with it before we get there. There's no need…'

There was a need, but as he glanced back at the Heads of State he knew his lawyer was right. To leave for such a reason could cause insupportable offence. It could cause powerful allies to turn to indifference.

His sense of helplessness was increasing almost to breaking point. *He couldn't protect his woman.*

'You can see, though,' Señor Rodriguez said, obviously realising just how he was torn. He turned back to the men and women behind him. 'If you'll excuse us for a moment,' he said smoothly. 'An urgent matter of security has come up. We'll be five minutes, no more.'

'I will go,' Ramón said through gritted teeth.

'It will be dealt with before you arrive,' Señor Rodriguez said again. 'But we have security monitors on the royal berth. I can switch our cameras there to reassure you until you see our security people take over. If you'll come aside…'

So Ramón followed the lawyer into an anteroom. He stared at the monitor in the corner, and he watched in grim desperation as his woman faced the press.

They'd pull her apart, he thought grimly—and there was nothing he could do to help her.

The cameras went wild. Questions were being shouted at her from all directions.

Courage, she told herself grimly. Come on, girl, you've hidden for long enough. Now's the time to stand and fight.

She ignored the shouts. She stood still and silent, knowing she looked appalling, knowing the shots would be of her at her worst. She'd just scrubbed out a boat. She didn't look like anyone famous. She was simply Jenny the deckhand, standing waiting for the shouting to stop.

And finally it did. The journalists fell silent at last, thinking she didn't intend to respond.

'Finished?' she asked, quirking an eyebrow in what she hoped looked like sardonic amusement, and the shouting started again.

Serenity, she told herself. She tapped a bare toe on the deck and waited again for silence.

'I've called His Highness,' Gordon called up from below. 'Security's on its way. Ramón'll send them.'

It didn't matter. This wasn't Ramón's fight, she thought. Finally, silence fell again; baffled silence. The cameras were still in use but the journalists were clearly wondering what they had here. She waited and they watched. Impasse.

'You do speak English?' one asked at last, a lone question, and she nodded. A lone question, not shouted, could be attended to.

And why not all the others, in serene order? Starting now.

'Yes,' she said, speaking softly so they had to stay silent or they couldn't hear her. 'I speak English as well as Spanish and French. My parents have Spanish blood. And I did indeed act as crew for His Highness, Prince Ramón, as we sailed between Sydney and Auckland.' She thought back through the questions that had been hurled at her, mentally ticking them off. 'Yes, I'm a cook. I'm… I *was* also a single mother. My son died of a heart condition two years ago, but I don't wish to answer any more questions about Matty. His death broke my heart. As for the rest… Thank you, I enjoyed last night, and yes, rumours that I cooked for His Highness early this morning are true. I'm employed as his cook and crew. That's what I've been doing for the last three months and no, I'm not sure if I'll continue. It depends if he needs me. What else? Oh, the personal questions. I'm twenty-nine years old. I had my appendix out when I was nine, my second toes are longer than my big toes and I don't eat cabbage. I think your country is lovely and the *Marquita* is the prettiest boat in the world.

However, scrubbing the *Marquita* is what I'm paid to do and that's what I'm doing. If you have any more questions, can you direct them to my secretary?'

She grinned then, a wide, cheeky grin which only she knew how much effort it cost to produce. 'Oh, whoops, I forgot I don't have a secretary. Can one of you volunteer? I'll pay you in muffins. If one of you is willing, then the rest can siphon your questions through him. That's so much more dignified than shouting, don't you think?'

Then she gave them all a breezy wave, observed their shocked silence and then slipped below, leaving them dumfounded.

She stood against the closed hatch, feeling winded. Gordon was staring at her in amazement. As well he might.

What was she doing?

Short answer? She didn't know.

Long answer? She didn't know either. Retiring from this situation with dignity was her best guess, though suddenly Jenny had no intention of retiring.

Not just yet.

This was a state-of-the-art security system, and sound was included. Not only did Ramón see everything, he heard every word Jenny spoke.

'It seems the lady doesn't need protecting,' Señor Rodriguez said, smiling his relief as Jenny disappeared below deck and Ramón's security guards appeared on the docks.

Ramón shook his head. 'I should have been there for her.'

'She's protected herself. She's done very well.'

'She shouldn't have been put in that position.'

'I believe the lady could have stayed below,' the lawyer said dryly. 'The lady chose to take them on. She has some courage.'

'She shouldn't...'

'She did,' the lawyer said, and then hesitated.

Señor Rodriguez had been watching on the sidelines for many years now. His father had been legal advisor to Ramón's grandmother, and Sofía had kept him on after Ramón's father died, simply to stay aware of what royalty was doing. Now he was doing the job of three men and he was thoroughly enjoying himself. 'Your Highness, if I may make so bold...'

'You've never asked permission before,' Ramón growled, and the lawyer permitted himself another small smile.

'It's just...the role you're taking on...to do it alone could well break you. You're allowing me to assist but no one else. This woman has courage and honour. If you were to...'

'I won't,' Ramón snapped harshly, guessing where the lawyer was going and cutting him off before he went any further. He flicked the screen off. There was nothing to see but the press, now being dispersed by his security guards. 'I do this alone or not at all.'

'Is that wise?'

'I don't know what's wise or not,' Ramón said and tried to sort his thoughts into some sort of sense. What was happening here? The lawyer was suggesting sharing the throne? With Jenny?

Jenny as his woman? Yes. But Jenny in the castle?

The thought left him cold. The night of his father's death was still with him, still haunting him.

Enough. 'We have work to do,' he growled and headed back to the room where the Heads of State were waiting.

'But...' the lawyer started, but Ramón was already gone.

CHAPTER TEN

HE MANAGED a few short words with her that night as he passed the supper room. It was all he had, as he moved from the evening's meetings to his briefing for tomorrow. To his surprise, Jenny seemed relaxed, even happy.

'I'm sorry about today,' he said. 'It seemed you handled things very well.'

'I talked too much,' she said, smiling. 'I need to work on my serenity.'

'Your serenity?'

'I'm not very good at it.' Her smile widened. 'But I showed promise today. Dr Matheson would be proud of me. By the way, I hope it's okay that Gordon and I are staying here tonight. The boat's up on the hard, and who wants to sleep on a boat in dry dock? Besides, staying in a palace is kind of fun.'

Kind of fun... He gazed into the opulent supper room, at the impassive staff, and he thought...*kind of fun*?

'So I can stay tonight?' she prompted.

He raked his hair. 'I should have had Señor Rodriguez organise airline tickets.'

'Señor Rodriguez has better things to do than organise my airline tickets. I'll organise them when I'm ready. Meanwhile, can I stay tonight?'

'Of course, but Jenny, I don't have time...'

'I know you don't,' she said sympathetically. 'Señor Rodrigucz says these first days are crazy. It'll get better, he says, but I'll not add to your burdens tonight. I hope I never will.'

Then, before he could figure how to respond, a servant appeared to remind him he was late for his next briefing. He was forced to leave Jenny, who didn't seem the least put out. She'd started chatting cheerfully to the maid who was clearing supper.

To his surprise, the maid was responding with friendliness and animation. Well, why wouldn't she, he told himself as he immersed himself again into royal business. Jenny had no baggage of centuries of oppression. She wasn't royal.

She never could be royal. He could never ask that of her, he thought grimly. But, as the interminable briefing wore on, he thought of Jenny—not being royal. He thought of her thinking of the palace as fun, and he almost told the suits he was talking to where to go.

But he didn't. He was sensible. He had a country to run, and when he was finally free Jenny had long gone to bed.

And there was no way he was knocking on her door tonight.

He missed her at breakfast, maybe because he ate before six before commencing the first of three meetings scheduled before ten. He moved through each meeting with efficiency and speed, desperate to find time to see her, but the meetings went overtime. He had no time left. His ten o'clock diary entry was immovable.

This appointment he'd made three months ago. Four hours every Wednesday. Even Jenny would have to wait on this.

Swiftly he changed out of his formal wear into jeans, grabbed his swimmers and made his way to the palace garages. He strode round the rows of espaliered fruit trees marking the end of the palace gardens—and Jenny was sitting patiently on a garden bench.

She was wearing smart new jeans, a casual cord jacket in a pale washed apricot over a creamy lace camisole and creamy leather ballet flats. Her curls were brushed until they shone. She looked rested and refreshed and cheerful.

She looked beautiful.

She rose and stretched and smiled a welcome. Gianetta.

Jenny, he told himself fiercely. This was Jenny, his guest before she left for ever.

A very lovely Jenny. Smiling and smiling.

'Do you like it?' she demanded and spun so she could be admired from all angles. 'This is the new smart me.'

'Where on earth…?'

'I went shopping,' she said proudly. 'Yesterday, when we finally escaped from that mob. Your security guys kindly escorted me to some great shops and then stood guard while I tried stuff on. Neat, yes?'

'Neat,' he said faintly and her face fell and he amended his statement fast. 'Gorgeous.'

'No, that won't do either,' she said reprovingly. 'My borrowed ball-gown was gorgeous. But this feels good. I thought yesterday I haven't had new clothes for years and the owner of the boutique gave me a huge discount.'

'I'll bet she did,' he said faintly.

She grinned. 'I know, it was cheeky, but I thought if I'm to be photographed by every cameraman in the known universe there has to be some way I can take advantage. She was practically begging me to take clothes.'

'Gordon said you were upset.'

'Gordon was upset.'

'I should have been there.'

'Then the cameramen would have been even more persistent,' she said gently. 'But I have clothes to face them now, and they're not so scary. So…I pinned Señor Rodriguez down this morning and he says you're going to see Philippe. So I was wondering…' Her tone became more diffident. 'Would it upset you if I came along? Would it upset Philippe?'

'No, but I can't ask you…'

'You're not asking,' she said and came forward to slip her

hands into his. 'You're looking trapped. I don't want you to feel that way. Not by me.'

'You'd never make me feel trapped,' he said. 'But Jenny, I can't expect…'

'Then don't expect,' she said. 'Señor Rodriguez told me all about Philippe. No, don't look like that. The poor man never had a chance; I practically sat on him to make him explain things in detail. Philippe's your cousin's son. Everyone thought he stood to inherit, only when his parents died it turned out they weren't actually married. According to royal rules, he's illegitimate. Now he has nothing.'

'He's well cared for. He has lovely foster parents.'

'Sofía says you've been visiting him every week since you got here.'

'It's the least I can do when he's lost his home as well as his parents.'

'He can't stay here?'

'No,' he said bleakly. 'If he's here he'll be in the middle of servants who'll either treat him like royalty—and this country hates royalty—or they'll treat him as an illegitimate nothing.'

'Yet you still think he should be here,' Jenny said softly.

'No.'

'Because this is where you were when your father died?'

'What the…?'

'Sofía,' she said simply. 'I asked, she told me. Ramón, I'm so sorry. It must have been dreadful. But that was then. Now is now. Can I meet him?'

'I can't ask that of you,' he said, feeling totally winded. 'And he's the same age your little boy would have been…'

'Ramón, can we take this one step at a time?' she asked. 'Let's just go visit this little boy—who's not Matty. Let's just leave it at that.'

So they went and for the first five miles or so they didn't speak. Ramón didn't know where to take this.

There were so many things in this country that needed his

attention but over and over his thoughts kept turning to one little boy. Consuela and Ernesto were lovely but they were in their sixties. To expect them to take Philippe long-term...

He glanced across at Jenny and found she was watching him. He had the top down on his Boxster coupe. The warm breeze was blowing Jenny's curls around her face. She looked young and beautiful and free. He remembered the trapped woman he'd met over three months ago and the change seemed extraordinary.

How could he trap her again? He couldn't. Of course he couldn't. He didn't intend to.

Yet—she'd asked to come. Was she really opening herself up to be hurt again?

'I can't believe this country,' she said, smiling, and he knew she was making an attempt to keep the conversation neutral. Steering away from undertones that were everywhere. 'It's like something on a calendar.'

'There's a deep description.'

'It's true. There's a calendar in the bathroom of Seaport Coffee 'n' Cakes and it has a fairy tale palace on it. All white turrets and battlements and moats, surrounded by little stone houses with ancient tiled roofs, and mountains in the background, and just a hint of snow.'

'There's no snow here,' he said, forced to smile back. 'We're on the Mediterranean.'

'Please,' she said reprovingly. 'You're messing with my calendar. So, as I was saying...'

But then, as he turned the car onto a dirt track leading to a farmhouse, she stopped with the imagery and simply stared. 'Where are we?'

'This is where Philippe lives.'

'But it's lovely,' she whispered, gazing out over grassy meadows where a flock of alpacas grazed placidly in the morning sun. 'It's the perfect place for a child to live.'

'He's not happy.'

'I imagine that might well be because his parents are dead,' she said, suddenly sharp. 'It'll take him for ever to adjust to their loss. If ever.'

'I don't think his parents were exactly hands-on,' Ramón told her. 'My uncle and my cousin liked to gamble, and so did Maria Therese. They spent three-quarters of their lives in Monaco and they never took Philippe. They were on their way there when their plane crashed.'

'So who took care of Philippe?'

'He's had a series of nannies. The palace hasn't exactly been a happy place to work. Neither my uncle nor my cousin thought paying servants was a priority, and I gather as a mother Maria Therese was…difficult. Nannies have come and gone.'

'So Philippe's only security has been the palace itself,' Jenny ventured.

'He's getting used to these foster parents,' Ramón said, but he wasn't convincing himself. 'They're great.'

'I'm looking forward to meeting them.'

'I'll be interested to hear your judgement.' Then he paused. 'Gianetta, are you sure you want to do this? Philippe's distressed and there's little I can do about it. It won't help to make you distressed as well. Would you like to turn back?'

'Well, that'd be stupid,' Jenny said. 'Philippe will already know you're on your way. To turn back now would be cruel.'

'But what about you?'

'This isn't about me,' she said, gently but inexorably. 'Let's go meet Philippe.'

He was the quietest little boy Jenny had ever met. He looked just like Ramón.

The family resemblance was amazing, she thought. Same dark hair. Same amazing eyes. Same sense of trouble, kept under wraps.

His foster parents, Consuela and Ernesto, were voluble and friendly. They seemed honoured to have Ramón visit, but not so overawed that it kept them silent. That was just as well, as their happy small talk covered up the deathly silence emanating from Philippe.

They sat at the farmhouse table eating Consuela's amazing strawberry cake. Consuela and Ernesto chatted, Ramón answered as best he could, and Jenny watched Philippe.

He was clutching a little ginger cat as if his life depended on it. He was too thin. His eyes were too big for his face.

He was watching his big cousin as if he was hungry.

I feel like that, she thought, and recognized what she'd thought and intensified her scrutiny. She had the time and the space to do it. Consuela and Ernesto were friendly but they were totally focused on Ramón. Philippe had greeted Jenny with courtesy but now he, too, was totally focused on Ramón.

Of course. Ramón was the Crown Prince.

Only Ramón's title didn't explain things completely, Jenny decided. Ramón was here in his casual clothes. He didn't look spectacular—or any more spectacular than he usually did—and a child wouldn't respond to an adult this way unless there was a fair bit of hero worship going on.

'Does Prince Ramón really come every week?' she asked Consuela as she helped clear the table.

'Every week since he's been back in the country,' the woman said. 'We're so grateful. Ernesto and I have had many foster children—some from very troubled homes—but Philippe's so quiet we don't seem to get through to him. He never says a thing unless he must. He hardly eats unless he's forced, and he certainly doesn't know how to enjoy himself. But once a week Ramón…I mean Crown Prince Ramón… comes and takes him out in his car and it's as if he lights up. He comes home happy, he eats, he tells us what he's done and he goes to bed and sleeps all night. Then he wakes and Ramón's not here, and his parents aren't here, and it all starts again. His Highness brought him his cat from the palace and that's made things better but now…we're starting to wonder if it's His Highness himself the child pines for.'

'He can't have become attached to Ramón so fast,' Jenny

said, startled, and Consuela looked at her with eyes that had seen a lot in her lifetime, and she smiled.

'*Caro*, are you telling me that's impossible?'

Oh, help, was she so obvious? She glanced back to where Ernesto and Ramón were engaged in a deep conversation about some obscure football match, with Philippe listening to every word as if it was the meaning of life—and she found herself blushing from the toes up.

'We're hearing rumours,' Consuela said, seemingly satisfied with Jenny's reaction. 'How lovely.'

'I…there's nothing.' *How fast did rumours spread?*

'There's everything,' Consuela said. 'All our prince needs is a woman to love him.'

'I'm not his class.'

'Class? Pah!' Consuela waved an airy hand at invisible class barriers. 'Three months ago Philippe was Prince Royal. Now he's the illegitimate son of the dead Prince's mistress. If you worry about class then you worry about nothing. You make him happy. That's all anyone can ask.' Her shrewd gaze grew intent. 'You know that Prince Ramón is kind, intelligent, honourable. Our country needs him so much. But for a man to take on such a role…there must be someone filling his heart as well.'

'I can't…'

'I can see a brave young woman before me, and I'm very sure you can.'

All of this was thoroughly disconcerting. She should just shut up, she thought. She should stick with her new found serenity. But, as she wiped as Consuela washed, she pushed just a little more. 'Can I ask you something?'

'Of course.'

'You and Ernesto… You obviously love Philippe and you're doing the best you can for him. But if Philippe wants to be at the palace… Why doesn't Ramón…why doesn't His Highness simply employ you to be there for him?'

The woman turned and looked at Jenny as if she were crazy. 'Us? Go to the palace?'

'Why not?'

'We're just farmers.'

'Um…excuse me. Didn't you just say…?'

'That's for you,' Consuela said, and then she sighed and dried her hands and turned to Jenny. 'I think that for you, you're young enough and strong enough to fight it, but for us…and for Philippe…the lines of class at the palace are immovable.'

'Would you try it, though?' she asked. 'Would you stay in the palace if Ramón asked it of you?'

'Maybe, but he won't. He won't risk it, and why should he?' She sighed, as if the worries of the world were too much for her, but then she pinned on cheerfulness, smiled determinedly at Jenny and turned back to the men. Moving on. 'Philippe. His Highness, Prince Ramón, asked if you could have your swimming costume prepared. He tells me he wishes to take you to the beach.'

Football was abandoned in an instant. 'In your car?' Philippe demanded of Ramón, round-eyed.

'In my car,' Ramón said. 'With Señorina Bertin. If it's okay with you.'

The little boy turned his attention to Jenny and surveyed her with grave attention. Whatever he saw there, it seemed to be enough.

'That will be nice,' he said stiffly.

'Get your costume, poppet,' Consuela said, but Philippe was already gone.

So they headed to the beach, about five minutes' drive from the farmhouse. Philippe sat between Jenny and Ramón, absolutely silent, his eyes straight ahead. But Jenny watched his body language. He could have sat ramrod still and not touched either of them, but instead he slid slightly to Ramón's side so his small body was just touching his big cousin.

Ramón was forging something huge here, Jenny thought. Did he know?

Maybe he did. Maybe he couldn't help but know. As he

drove he kept up a stream of light-hearted banter, speaking to Jenny, but most of what he said was aimed at Philippe.

Did Gianetta know this little car was the most wonderful car in the world? Did she know he thought this was the only one of its kind that had ever been fitted with bench seats—designed so two people could have a picnic in the car if it was raining? Why, only two weeks ago he and Philippe had eaten a picnic while watching a storm over the sea, and they'd seen dolphins. And now the bench seat meant there was room for the three of them. How about that for perfect? And it was red. Didn't Jenny think red was great?

'I like pink,' Jenny said, and Ramón looked as if she'd just committed blasphemy.

'You'd have me buy a pink car?'

'No, that'd be a waste. You could spray paint this one,' she retorted, and chuckled at their combined manly horror.

Philippe didn't contribute a word but she saw him gradually relax, responding to their banter, realizing that nothing was expected of him but that he relax and enjoy himself.

And he did enjoy himself. They arrived at the beach and Ramón had him in the water in minutes.

Jenny was slower. Señor Rodriguez had told her they often went swimming so she'd worn her bikini under her jeans, but for now she was content to paddle and watch.

The beach was glorious, a tiny cove with sun-bleached sand, gentle waves and shallow turquoise water. There were no buildings, no people and the mountains rose straight from the sea like sentinels guarding their privacy.

There'd be bodyguards. She'd been vaguely aware of cars ahead and behind them all day and shadowy figures at the farmhouse, but as they'd arrived at the beach the security presence was nowhere to be seen. The guards must be under orders to give the illusion of total privacy, she thought, and that was what they had.

Ramón had set this time up for Philippe. For a little cousin he was not beholden to in any way. A little boy who'd be miserable at the palace?

She paddled on, casually kicking water out in front of her, pretending she wasn't watching.

She was definitely watching.

Ramón was teaching Philippe to float. The little boy was listening with all the seriousness in the world. He was aching to do what his big cousin was asking of him. His body language said he'd almost die for his big cousin.

'If you float with your face in the water and count to ten, then I'll lift you out of the water,' Ramón was saying. 'My hand will be under your tummy until we reach ten and I'll count aloud. Then I'll lift you high. Do you trust me to do that?'

He received a solemn nod.

'Right,' Ramón said and Philippe leaned forward, leaned further so he was floating on Ramón's hand. And put his face in the water.

'One, two three…ten!' and the little boy was lifted high and hugged.

'Did you feel my hand fall away before I lifted you up? You floated? Hey, Gianetta, Philippe floated!' Ramón was spinning Philippe around and around until he squealed. His squeal was almost the first natural sound she'd heard from him. It was a squeal of delight, of joy, of life.

Philippe was just a little bit older than Matty would be right now. Ramón had worried about it. She'd dismissed his worry but now, suddenly, the knowledge hit her so hard that she flinched. She was watching a little boy learn to swim, and her Matty never would. Everything inside her seemed to shrink. Pain surged back, as it had surged over and over since she'd lost her little son.

But something about this time made it different. Something told her it must be different. So for once, somehow, she let the pain envelop her, not trying to deflect it, simply riding it out, letting it take her where it would. Trying to see, if she allowed it to take its course, whether it would destroy her or whether finally she could come out on the other side.

She was looking at a man holding a little boy who wasn't

Matty—a little boy who against all the odds, she was starting to care about.

The heart swells to fit all comers.

It was a cliché. She'd never believed it. Back at the hospital watching Matty fade, she'd looked at other children who'd come in ill, recovered then gone out again to face the world and she'd felt…nothing. It had been as if other children were on some parallel universe to the one she inhabited. There was no point of contact.

But suddenly, unbidden, those universes seemed to have collided. For a moment she thought the pain could make her head explode—and then she knew it wouldn't.

Matty. Philippe. Two little boys. Did loving Matty stop her feeling Philippe's pain?

Did loss preclude loving?

How could it?

She gazed out over the water, at this big man with the responsibilities of the world on his shoulders, and at this little boy whose world had been taken away from him.

She knew how many cares were pressing in on Ramón right now. He'd taken this day out, not for himself, but because he'd made a promise to Philippe. Every week, he'd come. Affairs of State were vital, but this, he'd decreed, was more so.

She thought fleetingly of the man who'd fathered Matty, who'd sailed away and missed his whole short life.

Philippe wasn't Ramón's son. He was the illegitimate child of a cousin he'd barely known and yet…and yet…

She was blinking back tears, struggling to take in the surge of emotions flooding through her, but slowly the knot of pain within was easing its grip, letting her see what lay past its vicious hold.

Ramón had lost his family and he'd been a loner ever since but now he was being asked to take on the cares of this country and the care of this little boy. This country depended on him. Philippe depended on him. But for him to do it alone…

Class barriers were just that, she thought. Grief was another barrier—and barriers could be smashed.

Could she face them all down?

Would Ramón want her to?

And if she did face them down for Ramón's sake, and for hers, she thought, for her thoughts were flowing in all sorts of tangents that hardly made sense, could she love Philippe as well? Could the knot of pain she'd held within since Matty's death be untied, maybe used to embrace instead of to exclude?

Her vision was blurred with tears and it was growing more blurred by the second. Ramón looked across at her and waved, as if to say, *what's keeping you; come in and join us*. She waved back and turned her back on them, supposedly to walk up the beach and strip off her outer clothes. In reality it was to get her face in order—and to figure if she had the courage to put it to the test.

Maybe they didn't want her. Maybe her instinctive feelings for Philippe were wrong, and maybe what Ramón was feeling for her stemmed from nothing more than a casual affair. Her heart told her it was much more, but then her heart was a fickle thing.

No matter. If she was mistaken she could walk away—but first she could try.

And Matty…

Surely loving again could never be a betrayal.

This was crazy, she told herself as she slipped off her clothes and tried to get her thoughts in order. She was thinking way ahead of what was really happening. She was imagining things that could never be.

Should she back off?

But then she glanced back at the two males in the shallows and she felt so proprietorial that it threatened to overwhelm her. My two men, she thought mistily, or they could be. Maybe they could be.

The country can have what it needs from Ramón but I'm lining up for my share, she told herself fiercely. If I have the courage. And maybe the shadows of Matty can be settled, warmed, even honoured by another love.

She sniffed and sniffed again, found a tissue in her bag, blew her nose and decided her face was in order as much as she could make it. She wriggled her bare toes in the sand and wriggled them again. If she dived straight into the waves and swam a bit to start with, she might even look respectable before she reached them.

And if she didn't...

Warts and all, she thought. That was what she was offering.

For they all had baggage, she decided, as she headed for the water. Her grief for Matty was still raw and real. This must inevitably still hurt.

And Ramón? He was an unknown, he was Crown Prince of Cepheus to her Jenny.

She was risking rejection, and everything that went with it.

Consuela said she had courage. Maybe Consuela was wrong.

'Maybe I'm just pig-headed stubborn,' she muttered to herself, heading into the shallows. 'Maybe I'm reading this all wrong and he doesn't want me and Philippe doesn't need me and today is all I have left of the pair of them.'

'So get in the water and get on with it,' she told herself.

'And if I'm right?'

'Then maybe serenity's not the way to go,' she muttered. 'Maybe the opposite's what's needed. Oh, but to fight for a prince...'

Maybe she would. For a prince's happiness.

And for the happiness of one small boy who wasn't Matty.

They swam, they ate a palace-prepared picnic on the sand and then they took a sleepy Philippe back to the farmhouse. Once again they drove in silence. What was between them seemed too complicated for words.

Dared she?

By the time they reached the farm, Philippe was asleep but,

as Ramón lifted him from the car, he jerked awake, then sobbed and clung. Shaken, Ramón carried him into the house, while Jenny stared straight ahead and wondered whether she could be brave enough.

It was like staring into the night sky, overwhelmed by what she couldn't see as much as what she could see. The concept of serenity seemed ridiculous now. This was facing her demons, fighting for what she believed in, fighting for what she knew was right.

Dared she?

Two minutes later Ramón was back. He slid behind the wheel, still without a word, and sat, grim-faced and silent.

Now or never. Jenny took a deep breath, reached over and put her hand over his.

'He loves you,' she whispered.

He stared down at their linked hands and his mouth tightened into a grim line of denial. 'He can't. If it's going to upset him then I should stop coming.'

'Do you want to stop?'

'No.'

'Then why not take him back to the palace? Why not take him home?'

There was a moment's silence. Then, 'What, take him back to the palace and wedge him into a few moments a day between my appointments? And the rest of the time?'

'Leave him with people who love him.'

'Like…'

'Like Consuela and Ernesto.' Then, at the look on his face, she pressed his hand tighter. 'Ramón, you're taking all of this on as it is. Why not take it as it could be?'

'I don't know what you mean.'

'Just try,' she said, figuring it out as she went. 'Try for change. You say the palace is a dreadful place to live. So it is, but the servants are terrified of your title. They won't let you close because they're afraid. The place isn't a home, it's a mausoleum. Oh, it's a gorgeous mausoleum but it's a mausoleum for all that. But it could change. People like Consuela and Ernesto could change it.'

'Or be swallowed by it.'

'There's no need to be melodramatic. You could just invite them to stay for a couple of days to start with. Tell Philippe that his home is here—make that clear so he won't get distraught if...*when* he has to return. You can see how it goes. You won't be throwing him back anywhere.'

'I won't make him sleep in those rooms.'

And there it was, out in the open, raw and dreadful as it had been all those years ago. And, even worse, Jenny was looking at him as if she understood.

And maybe she did.

'You were alone,' she whispered. ' Your father brought you to the palace and he was killed and you were alone.'

'It's nothing.'

'It's everything. Of course it is. But this is now, Ramón. This is Philippe. As it's not Matty, it's also not you. Philippe won't be alone.'

'This is nonsense,' he said roughly, trying to recover some sort of footing. 'It's impossible. Sofía saw that even before I arrived. Philippe's illegitimate. The country would shun him.'

'They'd love him, given half a chance.'

'How do you know?' he snapped. 'He was there for over four years and no one cared.'

'Maybe no one had a chance. The maid I talked to this morning said no one was permitted near except the nursery staff, and Philippe's mother was constantly changing the people who worked with him. He's better off here if no one loves him at the palace, of course he is. But you could change that.' She hesitated. 'Ramón, I'm thinking you already have.'

He shook his head, shaking off demons. 'This is nonsense. I won't risk *this*.'

'This?'

'You know what I mean.' His face grew even more strained. 'Gianetta...'

'Yes?'

'I hate it,' he said explosively. 'The paparazzi almost mobbed you yesterday. The threat from Carlos… How can anyone live in that sort of environment? How could you?'

Her world stilled. Her heart seemed to forget to beat. *How could you?* They were no longer talking about Philippe, then. 'Am I…am I being invited?' she managed.

'No!' There was a long silence, loaded with so many undercurrents she couldn't begin to figure them out. Through the silence Ramón held the steering wheel, his knuckles clenched white. Fighting demons she could hardly fathom.

'We need to get back,' he said at last.

'Of course we do,' she said softly, but she knew this man now. Maybe two weeks of living together was too soon to judge someone—or maybe not. Maybe she'd judged him the first time she'd seen him. Okay, she hardly understood his demons, but demons there were and, prince or not, maybe the leap had to be hers.

'You know that I love you,' she said gently into the warm breeze, but his expression became even more grim.

'Don't.'

'Don't say what I feel?'

'You don't want this life.'

'I like tiaras,' she ventured, trying desperately for lightness. 'And caviar and French champagne. At least,' she added honestly, 'I haven't tasted caviar yet, but I'm sure I'll like it. And if I don't, I'm very good at faking.'

'Jenny, don't make this any harder than it has to be,' he snapped, refusing to be deflected by humour. 'I was a fool to bring you to Cepheus. I will not drag you into this royal life.'

'You don't have to drag me anywhere. I choose where to go. All you need to do is ask.'

'Just leave it. You don't know… The paparazzi yesterday was just a taste. Right now you're seeing the romance, the fairy tale. You'll wake in a year's time and find nothing but a cage.'

'You don't think you might be overreacting?' she ventured. 'Not everyone at the Coronation ball looked like they've been locked up all their lives. Surely caviar can't be that bad.'

But he wasn't listening. 'You're my beautiful Jenny,' he said. 'You're wild and free, and I won't mess with who you are. You'll always be my Jenny, and I'll hold you in my heart for ever. From a distance.'

'From how big a distance? From a photo in a frame?' she demanded, indignant. 'That sounds appalling. Or, better still, do you mean as your mistress on your island?'

He stared at her as if she'd grown two heads. 'What the...?'

'That's what Sofía said we should do.'

'I do not want you as my mistress,' he said through gritted teeth.

'So you don't want me?' His anger was building, and she thought *good*. An angry Ramón might just lose control, and control had gone on long enough. She wanted him to take her into his arms. In truth she wanted him to take her any way he wanted, but he was fighting his anger, hauling himself back from the brink.

'I want you more than life itself, but I will not take you.' He took a deep ragged breath. 'I could never keep you safe.'

'Well, that's nonsense. I know karate,' she retorted. 'I can duck and I can run and I can even punch and scratch and yell if I need to. Not that I'll need to. Perpetua says Carlos is all bluster.'

'Perpetua...'

'Is a very nice lady with an oaf for a husband and with very old-fashioned ideas about royal wives shutting up. Ideas that I don't believe for one minute. You'll never see me shutting up.'

'It doesn't matter,' he said, exasperated. 'I want you free.'

'Free?' She was fighting on all fronts now, knowing only that she was fully exposed and she had no defence. All she had was her love for this man. 'Like our whale?' she demanded. 'That's just perspective. Our whale's free now to swim to Antarctica, but she has to stop there and turn around.

A minnow can feel free in an aquarium if it's a beautiful aquarium.'

She hesitated then, seeing the tension on his face stretched almost to breaking point. She'd gone far enough. 'Ramón, let's not take this further,' she said gently. 'What's between us…let's leave it for now. Let's just think of Philippe. Is his room still as it was at the palace?'

'No one's touched the nursery.'

'So you could go in right now and say, *Philippe, what about coming back to the palace for a night or two?* Tell him maybe if it works out he could come for two nights every week. See how it goes.'

'Jenny…'

'Okay, maybe it is impossible,' she said. 'This is not my life and it's not my little cousin. But you know him now, Ramón, and maybe things have changed. All I know is that Philippe's breaking his heart in there, and if he returned to the palace there's no way he'd be alone. Consuela is looking out the window and I wouldn't mind betting she knows exactly what we're talking about. She's bursting to visit the palace, even if she's scared, and if you raise one finger to beckon she'll have bags packed and Bebe in his cat crate and you can still reach your three o'clock appointment. And, before you start raising quibbles like who'll look after their alpacas, you're the prince, surely you can employ half this district to look after this farm. So decide,' she said bluntly. 'You've been making life and death decisions about this country. Now it's time to make one about your family.'

'Philippe's not my family.'

'Is he not? It might have started with sympathy, Ramón Cavellero, but it's not sympathy that's tugging him to you now. Is it?'

'I don't do…love.'

'You already have. Just take the next step. All it needs is courage.' She hesitated. 'Ramón, I know how it hurts to love and to lose. You've loved and you've lost, but Philippe is going right on loving.'

'He can't,' he said but he was looking at the window where Consuela was indeed peeping through a chink in the curtains.

And then he was looking at Jenny—Gianetta—who knew which?—and she was looking back at him with faith. Faith that he could take this new step.

'*You* can,' she said.

'Gianetta,' he said and would have taken her into his arms right then, part in exasperation, part in anger—and there were a whole lot more parts in there besides, but she held up her hands in a gesture of defence.

'Not me. Not now. This is you and Philippe. Do you want him or not?'

He looked at her for a long moment. He glanced back at the farmhouse, and Philippe was at the window now, as well as Consuela.

And there was only one answer to give.

So, half an hour later—Ramón would be late for his meeting but not much—his little red Boxster finally left the farmhouse, with Philippe once again snuggled between Ramón and Jenny. There was a cat crate at Jenny's feet. The Boxster was definitely crowded.

Behind them, Consuela and Ernesto drove their farm truck, packed with enough luggage to last them for two days.

Or more, Jenny thought with satisfaction. There were four big suitcases on the back. For all she talked of class differences, Consuela seemed more than prepared to take a leap into the unknown.

If only Ramón could join her.

CHAPTER ELEVEN

THE moment he swung back into the palace grounds affairs of State took over again. Ramón couldn't stay to watch Philippe's reaction to being back at the palace. He couldn't stay to see that Consuela and Ernesto were treated right.

He couldn't stay with Jenny.

'We can do this. Go,' Jenny told him and he had no choice. He went, to meeting upon interminable meeting. Once again he was forced to work until the small hours.

Finally, exhausted beyond belief, he made his way through the palace corridors towards his personal chambers. Once again he passed Jenny's door—and he didn't knock.

But then he reached the nursery. To his surprise, Manuel was standing outside the door, at attention. The footmen were posted at the top of the stairs. Had a change been ordered? But Manuel spoke before he could ask.

'I'm not permitted to move,' the man said, and it was as if a statue had come to life. 'But the little boy and Señorina Bertin... I thought you wouldn't wish them harm so I took it upon myself to stay here.'

'Good idea.' He hesitated, taking in the full context of what the man had said. Reaching the crux. 'Señorina Bertin's in there?'

'Yes, sir,' Manuel said and he opened the nursery door before Ramón could say he hadn't meant to go in; he was only passing.

Only of course he had meant to go in. Just to check.

Manuel closed the door after him. The room was in darkness but the moon was full, the curtains weren't drawn and he could see the outline of the bed against the windows. It was a truly vast bed for a small child. A ridiculous bed.

He moved silently across the room and looked down—and there were two mounds in the bed. A child-sized one, with a cat-shaped bump over his feet, and a Jenny-shaped one, and the Jenny-shaped one spoke.

'You're not a Hun?' she whispered, and he blinked.

'Pardon?'

'Manuel's saving us from the Huns. I thought you might have overpowered him and be about to…plunder and pillage. I'm very glad you're not.'

'I'm glad I'm not a Hun either,' he said and smiled down at her, and he could feel her smile back, even if he couldn't quite see it. 'What are you doing here?'

'Shh. He's only just gone back to sleep.'

He tugged a chair forward and sat, then leaned forward so he was inches away from Jenny's face. Philippe was separated from them by Jenny's body but he could see that her arm was around him. The sight made him feel…made him feel…

No. There were no words to describe it.

'This is Consuela's job,' he managed.

'She was here until midnight. The staff put Consuela and Ernesto into one of the state apartments, and it's so grand it's made Ernesto quiver. Ernesto seems more frightened than Philippe so I said I'd stay.'

She said she'd stay. With a little boy who was the same age as her Matty. In this room that he'd once slept in. He looked at her, at the way Philippe's body was curved against hers, at the way she was holding him, and he felt things slither and change within him. Knots that had been around his heart for ever slipped away, undone, free.

'Gianetta…' he whispered and placed his fingers on her lips, wondering. If she'd found the courage to do this…

'Shh,' she said again. 'He woke and he was a little upset. I don't want him to wake again.'

'But you soothed him.'

'I told him the story of the whale. He loved it. I told him about his cousin, the hero, saviour of whales. Saviour of this country. We both thought it was pretty cool.'

'Gianetta…'

'Jenny. Your employee. And Manuel is out there.'

'Manuel can go…'

'Manuel can't go,' she said seriously. 'Neither of us is sure where to take this. You need to sleep, Ramón.'

'I want…'

'I know,' she said softly and she placed a finger on his lips in turn. 'We both want. I can feel it, and it's wonderful. But there's things to think about for both of us. For now… Give me my self-respect and go to your own bedroom tonight.' She smiled at him then and he was close enough to see a lovely loving smile that made his heart turn over. 'Besides,' she said. 'Tonight I'm sleeping with Philippe. One man a night, my love. I have my reputation to think of.'

'He's not Matty,' he said before he could stop himself.

'Philippe's not Matty, no.'

'But… Jenny, doesn't that tear you in two?'

'I thought it would,' she said on a note of wonder. 'But now… He fits exactly under my arm. He's not Matty but it's as if Matty has made a place for him. It feels right.'

'Jenny…'

'Go to bed, Ramón,' she said simply. 'We all have a lot of thinking to do this night.'

He left and she was alone in the dark with a sleeping child. She'd given her heart, she thought. She'd given it to both of them, just like that.

What if they didn't want it?

It was theirs, she thought, like it or not.

Bebe stirred and wriggled and padded his way up the bed

to check she was still breathing, that she'd still react if he kneaded his paws on the bedcover.

'Okay, I can learn to love you, too,' she told the little cat. 'As long as your claws don't get all the way through the quilt.' Satisfied, Bebe slumped down on the coverlet across her breast and went back to sleep, leaving her with her thoughts.

'They have to want me,' she whispered in the dark. 'Oh, they have to want me or I'm in such big trouble.'

And in the royal bedchamber, the apartment of the Crown Prince of Cepheus, there was no sleep at all.

Once upon a time a child had slept alone in this palace and known terror. Now the man lay alone in his palace and knew peace.

He woke and he knew, but he couldn't do a thing about it.

It'd take him a week, Señor Rodriguez told him, this signing, signing and more signing. He had to formally accept the role of Crown Prince before he could begin to delegate, so from dawn his time was not his own.

'I need two hours this afternoon,' he growled to his lawyer as he saw his packed diary. 'You've scheduled me an hour for lunch. Take fifteen minutes from each delegation; that gives me another hour, so between one and three is mine.'

'I've already started organising it,' his lawyer told him. 'We all want you to have time with the child.'

'All?'

'I believe the staff have been missing him,' the lawyer said primly. 'It seems there are undercurrents neither the Princess Sofía nor I guessed.'

He didn't say more, but they agreed a message would be sent to Jenny and to Philippe that he'd spend the early afternoon with them. Then Ramón put his head down and worked.

He finished just before one. He'd have finished earlier only someone dared ask a question. Was he aware there were up to fifty students in each class in the local schools, and didn't he agree this was so urgent it had to be remedied right now?

He did agree. How could he put his own desire to be with Jenny and Philippe before the welfare of so many other children? Señor Rodriguez disappeared, leaving Ramón to listen and think and agree to meet about the issue again tomorrow. Finally he was free to walk out, to find the whereabouts of Philippe…and of Jenny.

'They're by the pool, Your Highness.' It was the maid who normally brought in his coffee and, to his astonishment, she smiled as she bobbed her normal curtsy. 'It's so good to have him back sir. There's refreshments being served now. If you'd like to have your lunch with them…'

Bemused, he strolled out the vast palace doors into the gardens overlooking the sea.

There was a party happening by the pool, and the perfection of the scene before him was marred. Or not marred, he corrected himself. Just changed.

The landscape to the sea had been moulded to create a series of rock pools and waterfalls tumbling down towards the sea. Shade umbrellas and luxurious cream beach loungers were discreetly placed among semi-tropical foliage, blending unobtrusively into the magical garden setting.

Now, however… At the biggest rock pool chairs and tables had been hauled forward to make a circle. There were balloons attached around every umbrella. This wasn't tasteful at all, he thought with wry amusement. The balloons were all colours and sizes, as though some had been blown up by men with good lungs, and some had been blown up by a five-year-old. They were attached to the umbrellas by red ribbons, with vast crimson bows under each bunch.

And there were sea dragons floating in the rock pool. Huge plastic sea dragons, red, green and pink, with sparkly tiaras. Sea dragons with tiaras? What on earth…?

Jenny was in the water, and so was Philippe and so was…Sofía? They were on a sea dragon apiece, kicking their way across the water, seemingly racing. Sofía was wearing neck to knee swimmers and she was winning, whooping her elderly lungs out with excitement.

There was more, he thought, stunned. Señor Rodriguez was sitting by the edge of the pool, wearing shorts, his skinny frame a testament to a life spent at his desk. He was cheering Sofía at full roar. As were Consuela and Ernesto, yelling their lungs out for their foster son. 'Go, Philippe, go!'

There were also servants, all in their ridiculous uniforms, but each of them was yelling as loudly as everyone else. And another woman was cheering too, a woman who looked vaguely familiar. And then he recognised her. Perpetua. Carlos's wife! What the…?

He didn't have time to take it all in. Sofía reached the wall by a full length of sea dragon. Philippe came second and Jenny fell off her dragon from laughing.

It felt crazy. It was a palace transformed into something else entirely. He watched as Philippe turned anxiously to find Jenny. She surfaced, still laughing, she hugged him and his heart twisted and he forgot about everything, everyone else.

She saw him. She waved and then staggered—holding Philippe with one arm was a skill yet to be mastered. 'Welcome to our pool party, Your Highness,' she called. 'Have you come to try our sausage rolls?'

'Sausage rolls,' he said faintly, and looked at the table where there was enough food for a small army.

'Your chefs have never heard of sausage rolls,' she said, clambering up the pool steps with Philippe in her arms and grinning as Sofía staggered out as well, still clutching her sea dragon. 'Philippe and I had to teach them. And we have fairy bread and lamingtons, and tacos and tortillas and strawberries and éclairs—and I love this place. Philippe does too, don't you Philippe? We've decided it's the best place to visit in the world.'

Visit. He stood and watched as woman and child disappeared under vast towels and he thought…*visit*.

'Oh, and we invited Perpetua,' Jenny said from under her towel, motioning in the general direction of the pallid little lady standing uncertainly under the nearest umbrella.

Perpetua gave him a shy, scared smile. 'You know Carlos's wife? And Carlos, too.'

'And Carlos, too?' he demanded. Perpetua's smile slipped.

'I told him to come,' she whispered. 'When Gianetta invited us. He said he would. He just has to...he's been making silly threats that he doesn't mean. He wants to apologise.' Her voice was almost pleading. 'He'd never hurt...'

And maybe he wouldn't, Ramón thought. For Carlos was approaching them now, escorted by palace footmen. The footmen were walking really close. Really close.

'He's not going to hurt anyone,' Perpetua whispered. 'He's just been silly. I was so pleased when Gianetta rang. He needs a chance to explain.'

'Explain what?' Ramón said and Perpetua fell silent, waiting for Carlos himself to answer.

Ramón's gaze flew to Jenny. She met his gaze full on. She'd set this up, he thought.

One of the maids had taken over rubbing Philippe dry. The maid was laughing and scolding, making Philippe smile back. She was a servant he'd thought lacked emotion.

Had the servants turned to ice through mistreatment and fear?

What else had fear done?

He looked again at Carlos, a big, stupid man who for a few short weeks, while Ramón couldn't be found, had thought the throne was his. For the dream to be snatched away must have shattered his world.

Maybe stupid threats could be treated as they deserved, Ramón thought, feeling suddenly extraordinarily light-headed. And if threats weren't there...

'We invited both Carlos and Perpetua,' Jenny was saying. 'Because of Philippe. Philippe says Perpetua's always been nice to him.'

'He's a sweetheart,' Perpetua said stoutly, becoming braver. 'I worried about him whenever I stayed here.'

'You used to stay in the palace?' Ramón asked, surprised again. What had Señor Rodriguez told him? Perpetua was a nice enough woman, intelligent, trained as a grade school teacher, but always made to feel inferior to Carlos's royal relatives.

'A lot,' Perpetua said, becoming braver. 'Carlos liked being here. Philippe and I became friends, didn't we, sweetheart. But then Carlos said some silly things.' Her gaze met her husband's. 'I used to believe…well, I'm a royal wife and a royal wife stays silent. But Gianetta says that's ridiculous. So I'm not staying silent any longer. You're sorry, aren't you, dear?'

Was he? Ramón watched Carlos, sweating slightly in a suit that was a bit too tight, struggling to come to terms with this new order, and he even felt a bit sorry for him.

'I shouldn't have said it,' Carlos managed.

'You said you'd kill…'

'You know how it is.' Carlos was almost pleading. 'I mean…heat of the moment. I was only saying…you know, wild stuff. What I'd do if you didn't look after the country… that sort of thing. It got blown up. You didn't take it seriously. Please tell me you didn't take it seriously.'

Was that it? Ramón thought, relief running through him in waves. History had created fear—not fear for himself but fear for family. His family.

A family he could now build. In time…

And with that thought came another. He wasn't alone.

Delegation. Why not start now?

'Perpetua, you used to be a grade teacher,' he said, speaking slowly but thinking fast, thinking back to the meeting he'd just attended. 'Do you know the conditions in our schools?'

'Of course I do,' Perpetua said, confused. 'I mean, I haven't taught for twenty years—Carlos doesn't like me to—but I have friends who are still teachers. They have such a hard time…'

'Tomorrow morning I'm meeting with a deputation to see what can be done about the overcrowding in our classrooms,' he said. 'Would you like to join us?'

'Me?' she gasped.

'I need help,' he said simply. 'And Carlos… How can you help?'

There was stunned silence. Even Philippe, who was wrapped in a towel and was now wrapping himself around a sausage roll stopped mid-bite and stared. This man who'd made blustering threats to kill…

How can you help?

Jenny moved then, inconspicuously slipping to his side. She stood close and she took his hand, as if she realized just how big it was. Just how important this request was.

Defusing threats to create a future.

Refusing to stand alone for one moment longer.

'I can't…' Carlos managed at last. 'There's nothing.'

'Yes, dear, there is.' Perpetua had found her voice, and she, too, slipped to stand beside her man. 'Sports. Carlos loves them, loves watching them, but there's never been enough money to train our teenagers. And the football stadium's falling down.'

'You like football?' Ramón asked.

'Football,' Philippe said, lighting up.

'I…'

'You could give me reports on sports facilities,' Ramón said, thinking fast, trying to figure out something meaningful that the man could do. 'Tell me what needs to be done. Put in your recommendations. I don't know this country. You do. I need help on the ground. So what do we have here? Assistant to the Crown for Education. Assistant to the Crown for Sport.'

'And I'll be Assistant to the Crown for New Uniforms for The Staff,' Sofía said happily. 'I'd like to help with that.'

'I can help with floating,' Philippe said gamely. 'But can I help with football, too?'

'And Gianetta?' Perpetua said, looking anxious. 'What about Jenny?'

'I need to figure that out,' Ramón said softly, holding his love close, his world suddenly settling in a way that was leaving him stunned. 'In private.'

Philippe had finished his sausage roll now, and he carried the loaded tray over to his big cousin.

'Would you like to eat one?' he asked. 'And then will you teach me to float some more?'

'Of course I will,' he said. 'On one condition.'

Philippe looked confused, as well he might.

No matter. Sometimes a prince simply had to allocate priorities, and this was definitely that time. He tugged Jenny tighter, then, audience or not, he pulled her into his arms and gave her a swift possessive kiss. It was a kiss that said he was pushed for time. He knew he couldn't take this further, not here, not now, but there was more where that came from.

'My condition to you all,' he said softly, kissing her once more, a long lingering kiss that said, pushed for time or not, this was what he wanted most in the world, 'is that Señor Rodriguez changes my diary. This night is mine.'

The car came to collect her just before sunset. She was dressed again as Gianetta, in a long diaphanous dress made of the finest layers of silk and chiffon with the diamonds at her throat. Two maids and Sofía and Consuela and Perpetua had clucked over her to distraction. Sofía had added a diamond bracelet of her own, and had wept a little.

'Oh, my dear, you're so beautiful,' she'd said mistily. 'Do you think he'll propose?'

Jenny hadn't answered. She couldn't. She was torn between laughter and tears.

Ramón's kisses had promised everything, but nothing had been said. Mistress to a Crown Prince? Wife?

Dared she think wife?

How could she think anything? After a fast floating lesson Ramón had been swept away yet again on his interminable business and she'd been left only with his demand.

'A car will come for you at seven. Be ready.'

She was ready, but she was daring to think nothing.

Finally, at seven the car came and Señor Rodriguez handed her into the limousine with care and with pride. The reverberations from this afternoon were being felt all around the country, and the lawyer couldn't stop smiling.

'Where's Ramón?' she managed.

'Waiting for you,' the lawyer said, sounding inscrutable until he added, 'How could any man not?'

So she was driven in state, alone, with only a chauffeur for company. The great white limousine was driven slowly through the city, out along the coast road, up onto a distant headland where it drew to a halt.

Two uniformed footmen met her, Manuel and Luis, trying desperately to be straight-faced. There was a footpath leading from where the car pulled in to park, winding through a narrow section of overgrown cliff. Manuel and Luis led her silently along the path, emerged into a clearing, then slipped silently back into the shadows. Leaving her to face what was before her.

And what was before her made her gasp. A headland looking out all over the moonlit Mediterranean. A table for two. Crisp white linen. Two cushioned chairs with high, high backs, draped all in white velvet, each leg fastened with crimson ties.

Silverware, crystal, a candelabrum magnificent enough to take her breath away.

Soft music coming from behind a slight rise. Real music. *There were real musicians somewhere behind the trees.*

Champagne on ice.

And then Ramón stepped from the shadows, Ramón in full ceremonial, Ramón looking more handsome than any man she'd met.

The sound of frogs came from beneath the music behind him. Her frog prince?

'If I kiss you, will you join your friends, the frogs?' she whispered before she could help herself and he laughed and came towards her and took her hands in his.

'No kissing,' he said tenderly. 'Not yet.'

'What…?' She could barely speak. 'What are we waiting for?'

'This,' he said and went down on bended knee.

She closed her eyes. This couldn't be happening.

This was happening.

'This should wait until after dinner,' he said softly, 'but it's been burning a hole in my pocket for three hours now.' And, without more words, he lifted a crimson velvet box and held it open. A diamond ring lay in solitary splendour, a diamond so wonderful...so amazing...

'Is it real?' she gasped and he chuckled.

'That's Jenny speaking. I think we need Gianetta to give us the right sense of decorum.'

Gianetta. She took a deep breath and fought for composure. She could do this.

'Sire, you do me honour.'

'That's more like it,' he said and his dark eyes gleamed with love and with laughter. 'So, Gianetta, Jenny, my love, my sailor, my cook extraordinaire, my heart...I give you my love. The past has made us solitary, but it's up to both of us to move forward. To leave solitude and pain behind. You've shown me courage, and I trust that I can match it. So Gianetta, my dearest love, if I promise to love you, cherish you, honour you, for as long as we both shall live, will you do me the honour of taking my hand in marriage?'

She looked down into his loving eyes. Then she paused for a moment, taking time to gaze around her, at the night, at the stars, the accoutrements of royalty, at the lights of Cepheus glowing around them. Knowing also there was a little boy waiting as well.

Her family. Her love, starting now.

'I believe I will,' she said gently and, before he could respond, she dropped to her own knees and she took his hands in hers.

'Yes, my love and my prince, I believe I will.'

HARLEQUIN *Romance*

Coming Next Month

Available September 14, 2010

#4189 AUSTRALIA'S MOST ELIGIBLE BACHELOR
Margaret Way
The Rylance Dynasty

#4190 PASSIONATE CHEF, ICE QUEEN BOSS
Jennie Adams
The Brides of Bella Rosa

#4191 ACCIDENTALLY PREGNANT!
Rebecca Winters
Mediterranean Dads

#4192 SPARKS FLY WITH MR. MAYOR
Teresa Carpenter

#4193 WEDDING DATE WITH THE BEST MAN
Melissa McClone
Girls' Weekend in Vegas

#4194 DESERTED ISLAND, DREAMY EX!
Nicola Marsh
The Fun Factor

REQUEST YOUR FREE BOOKS!
2 FREE NOVELS PLUS 2
FREE GIFTS!

HARLEQUIN® *Romance*®

From the Heart, For the Heart

YES! Please send me 2 FREE Harlequin® Romance novels and my 2 FREE gifts (gifts are worth about $10). After receiving them, if I don't wish to receive any more books, I can return the shipping statement marked "cancel". If I don't cancel, I will receive 6 brand-new novels every month and be billed just $3.32 per book in the U.S. or $3.72 per book in Canada. That's a savings of at least 26% off the cover price! It's quite a bargain! Shipping and handling is just 50¢ per book.* I understand that accepting the 2 free books and gifts places me under no obligation to buy anything. I can always return a shipment and cancel at any time. Even if I never buy another book, the two free books and gifts are mine to keep forever.

116/316 HDN E5NS

Name _____ (PLEASE PRINT) _____

Address _____ Apt. # _____

City _____ State/Prov. _____ Zip/Postal Code _____

Signature (if under 18, a parent or guardian must sign) _____

Mail to the **Harlequin Reader Service:**
IN U.S.A.: P.O. Box 1867, Buffalo, NY 14240-1867
IN CANADA: P.O. Box 609, Fort Erie, Ontario L2A 5X3

Not valid for current subscribers to Harlequin Romance books.

**Are you a subscriber to Harlequin Romance books
and want to receive the larger-print edition?
Call 1-800-873-8635 today!**

* Terms and prices subject to change without notice. Prices do not include applicable taxes. Sales tax applicable in N.Y. Canadian residents will be charged applicable provincial taxes and GST. Offer not valid in Quebec. This offer is limited to one order per household. All orders subject to approval. Credit or debit balances in a customer's account(s) may be offset by any other outstanding balance owed by or to the customer. Please allow 4 to 6 weeks for delivery. Offer available while quantities last.

Your Privacy: Harlequin Books is committed to protecting your privacy. Our Privacy Policy is available online at www.eHarlequin.com or upon request from the Reader Service. From time to time we make our lists of customers available to reputable third parties who may have a product or service of interest to you. If you would prefer we not share your name and address, please check here. ☐

Help us get it right—We strive for accurate, respectful and relevant communications. To clarify or modify your communication preferences, visit us at www.ReaderService.com/consumerschoice.

HR10R

HARLEQUIN®

A *Romance*

FOR EVERY MOOD™

Spotlight on

— Heart & Home —

Heartwarming romances
where love can happen
right when you least expect it.

See the next page to enjoy a sneak peek
from Harlequin Superromance®,
a Heart and Home series.

Enjoy a sneak peek at fan favorite Molly O'Keefe's
Harlequin Superromance miniseries,
THE NOTORIOUS O'NEILLS, *with*
TYLER O'NEILL'S REDEMPTION,
available September 2010
only from Harlequin Superromance.

Police chief Juliette Tremblant recognized the shape of the man strolling down the street—in as calm and leisurely fashion as if it were the middle of the day rather than midnight. She slowed her car, convinced her eyes were playing tricks on her. It had been a long time since Tyler O'Neill had been seen in this town.

As she pulled to a stop at the curb, he turned toward her, and her heart about stopped.

"What the hell are you doing here, Tyler?"

"Well, if it isn't Juliette Tremblant." He made his way over to her, then leaned down so he could look her in the eye. He was close enough to touch.

Juliette was not, repeat, *not* going to touch Tyler O'Neill. Not with her fingers. Not with a ten-foot pole. There would be no touching. Which was too bad, since it was the only way she was ever going to convince herself the man standing in front of her—as rumpled and heart-stoppingly handsome now as he'd been at sixteen—was real.

And not a figment of all her furious revenge dreams.

"What are you doing back in Bonne Terre?" she asked.

"The manor is sitting empty," Tyler said and shrugged, as though his arriving out of the blue after ten years was casual. "Seems like someone should be watching over the family home."

"You?" She laughed at the very notion of him being here for any unselfish reason. "Please."

He stared at her for a second, then smiled. Her heart fluttered against her chest—a small mechanical bird powered by that smile.

"You're right." But that cryptic comment was all he offered.

Juliette bit her lip against the other questions.

Why did you go?

Why didn't you write? Call?

What did I do?

But what would be the point? Ten years of silence were all the answer she really needed.

She had sworn off feeling anything for this man long ago. Yet one look at him and all the old hurt and rage resurfaced as though they'd been waiting for the chance. That made her mad.

She put the car in gear, determined not to waste another minute thinking about Tyler O'Neill. "Have a good night, Tyler," she said, liking all the cool "go screw yourself" she managed to fit into those words.

It seems Juliette has an old score to settle with Tyler.
Pick up TYLER O'NEILL'S REDEMPTION
to see how he makes it up to her.
Available September 2010,
only from Harlequin Superromance.

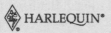
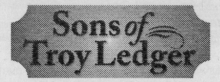

HARLEQUIN® Romance®

MARGARET WAY

introduces

THE *Rylance* DYNASTY

**The lives & loves of
Australia's most powerful family**

Growing up in the spotlight hasn't been easy, but the two
Rylance heirs, Corin and his sister, Zara, have come of age
and are ready to claim their inheritance. Though they are
privileged, proud and powerful, they are about to discover
that there are some things money can't buy....

Look for:

Australia's Most Eligible Bachelor
Available September

Cattle Baron Needs a Bride
Available October

HR17679